AVA OLSEN

EVERNIGHT PUBLISHING ®

www.evernightpublishing.com

Copyright© 2022

Ava Olsen

ISBN: 978-0-3695-0672-6

Cover Artist: Jay Aheer

Editor: Jessica Ruth

AVA OLSEN

DEDICATION

For my mother, who is never without a book.

AVA OLSEN

NOVEL AFFAIR

NY Nights, 1

Ava Olsen

Copyright © 2022

Chapter One
Ryker

"A writing partner? No fucking way! I am not collaborating with a phony-ass fame chaser like Wes Stewart. I work alone, end of!"

Ryker Desoumas stopped yelling to take a deep breath and pace the hardwood floors in his New York City loft, counting down from a hundred in his head to calm the rush of anger and anxiety that raced through his body.

Despite his success as a science fiction author, he was still a neurotic mess for the most part. Or maybe that was why he was such a prolific writer—he had so much crap in his brain to work through. As an introvert, a workaholic, and a self-admitted grumpy pain in the ass, he was best left alone. He kept to himself, his work, a few close friends and family, his pets, and the occasional hook-up with a hot man when he needed it. What more could a thirty-three-year-old gay man want?

His friend and publisher, McIntyre Duran,

chuckled on the other end of the line. Mac was a charming bastard, but wily as hell. The cool negotiator could convince anyone to do just about anything, and Ryker was next on his hit list. That low, rumbling laugh of Mac's meant he was up to no good and plotting his next move.

"Phony-ass fame chaser? Man, you should use that line in your next book. That's fucking awesome!" Mac continued to laugh for a bit, then cleared his throat. "But seriously, Ry, this is an amazing opportunity. I liked the first draft of *1,000 Days of the Darkest Planet*, but maybe it's time to switch it up. I know you've wanted to write a fantasy series with a gay romance angle for a while now, and here's your chance. With both your names attached, it will sell to a wide audience, maybe even snag a movie deal. Wes Stewart is a celebrity author. Between his mysteries and non-fiction books, he's an international bestseller. Reputation and visibility equals success. Mainstream literature and media need more gay relationship representation. You and I have talked about this."

Ryker and Mac both came out in their teens. While Ryker's mother had always supported and loved him, Mac had not been so lucky. Mac no longer spoke to his very wealthy extended family, with the exception of his grandfather.

Ryker sighed and ran a hand over his three-day stubble. "Look, Mac, I want to write that series, but I work alone. I haven't collaborated on anything since I worked at the *Evening Post*. And that didn't end well, as you know." He paused, shivering.

Thinking back to his days as a crime reporter was not a pleasant trip down memory lane. Whenever snippets of that life entered his thoughts, the nightmares returned. Mac knew the gist of what had happened to

Ryker during that period in his life, but the details remained in Ryker's mind, only to be shared with a shrink.

Running his fingers up his face and through his long black hair, Ryker paced again, glancing at the whiteboard hanging on the wall beside his desk. Book ideation was a unique process for every writer, and Ryker was no different. He started with his board, adding copious notes, pictures, and other items for inspiration and brainstorming. Then he moved into his organized chaos of character development and plotting. Looking at it now, he couldn't imagine how he'd work with someone else.

"You could end up with a real-life murder story on your hands if I have to partner with someone else, especially Wesley Stewart," Ryker said. "From what I've heard, he's a charming, self-promoting tool. I'm a curmudgeon at the best of times. How's that gonna work?"

Shaking his head, he walked over to his desk with the view overlooking Central Park and glanced out the window. The spectacular scene of the city below made his breath catch every time. Then his gaze caught on his tired reflection—shoulder-length black hair, beard scruff, and blue eyes with even bluer circles under them. He wore his usual uniform of ripped jeans, black t-shirt, and dark-framed glasses. After several nights of working rather than sleeping, he was in dire need of rest. And a haircut. But why bother when he'd be stuck here for another week revising the first draft of his latest work in progress? Who did he need to impress?

"Jesus, Ry, you're already dismissing the idea when you haven't even sat down with us to discuss it and meet Wes in person. I know you're opposites, personality-wise, but he's a great writer. He's versatile and has a huge fan base. Combining your talents could result in amazing things. He's thrilled about a gay fiction series. He wants it to reach a large audience, something with depth and substance, and you can bring that." Mac finished his response with so much passion Ryker put the call on speakerphone and clapped as the audience of one.

"Nice pitch, Mac. Bravo. And to your point, considering the self-help bullshit he peddles now, he's badly in need of substance and depth," Ryker replied sarcastically, crossing his arms and eyeing the phone in front of him. Christ, just the thought of upending his routine by having to work with anyone, especially an attention-loving narcissist, was making him sweat like a five-mile run.

Despite his snarky comment, Ryker pondered how to handle this situation. One teeny, tiny part of him was a little bit intrigued. Like an inch. Maybe two.

He would never admit to Mac that he had secretly read a few of Wes's fiction books and they were pretty damn good. Intriguing plots with witty dialogue from a recurring character that made him laugh out loud—light, entertaining reads when you needed to unwind. But vastly different to Ryker's novels in terms of the tone and length. And just because he enjoyed reading Wes Stewart's books didn't mean Ryker could—or should—work with him.

"And, Mac, he's happy right now because he hasn't met me yet. All he knows about me is what's written on the book jacket, which is not much, considering I write under a pen name. I'm a fucking hermit compared to him! I'm not in this business to have my life plastered on the news, like he is." He paused and lowered his voice to a low grumble. "So forget it. Murder He Wrote can go find another writer to work with." Ryker sat his ass down on the royal-blue sectional and took a deep breath.

"Ry, I'm asking you, as my friend, to keep an open mind about this. Please? Look, I have another meeting, so I gotta go, but we'll talk more about this at dinner on Saturday, okay? You are still planning to be there, right?" Mac asked.

Mac held monthly dinner parties for his friends and business contacts, and there was always an eclectic mix of guests, which made for interesting conversation. Mac was generous and welcoming, and Ryker appreciated that he was always included. Ryker could handle dinner parties with limited guests, but big events were usually a no.

Much as he hated socializing, Ryker wouldn't refuse Mac's request. He wasn't vocal about how much his closest friends meant to him, but he would always be loyal to them in whatever way he could. They had been through the good and the bad together over the years, and he would stick by them no matter what.

"Yes, of course I'll be there. Is Cal going?" Ryker asked.

Callum Pattison was a mutual friend and a mixed medium artist and illustrator. His work had recently picked up the attention of established patrons in New York and beyond. Besides his own work, Cal designed Ryker's book covers.

Ryker was both in awe and slightly envious of his two closest friends and their ability to connect so easily with others. Ryker was always too much in his head to relax in social situations. Unless he had a drink or several in him, which didn't happen often. At least, it hadn't for a long time.

He had a curious feeling that might change Saturday night.

"Yes, Cal will be there to keep everyone

entertained with his travel stories and unusual sexcapades. Shit, you never know what's going to come out of that mouth of his," Mac replied, laughing. Cal did not hide anything—his bisexuality, his opinions, or any thought he had about, well, anything.

Ryker sighed. "Better him than me. But I'll do my best to socialize despite my grumpy demeanor," he said. Ryker knew Mac well enough to bet he was now rolling his eyes. Ryker wondered how many people would be attending, but Mac was cryptic about details. "And at dinner, don't sit me next to anyone who works in media or public relations or…"

Mac interrupted Ryker. "Yes, bud, I know the drill. Just come and enjoy yourself, okay? You need some human interaction. I haven't seen you in three weeks, and I worry. You get so wrapped up in your work, you don't do anything else." Mac's voice was suddenly muffled, like he'd covered the receiver to speak to someone else. "Sorry about that, but my other meeting starts in a few minutes. Talk soon, okay?"

"Later, Mac."

Ryker placed his phone on the arm of the sofa, crossing his left foot to rest on his right knee, his leg bouncing up and down. A prickle of unease crept up his spine and radiated into the back of his head.

Schmoozing at dinner parties and book collaborations. Fuck me! Ryker thought as he placed his hands over his face and wondered what else was next.

He continued his deep-breathing ritual, and his tension eased.

Ryker glanced around and took in the stillness of the apartment he loved, his perfect sanctuary. After his third bestseller, he'd splurged on a penthouse apartment on Park Avenue, and given that he spent most of his time here writing, it was well worth it.

The whitewashed wood floors complemented the dark gray feature wall that was full of artwork (including Cal's, of course) and photos of his family and friends. The kitchen was compact but well-appointed with a large breakfast bar. Slate-blue cabinets combined with polished concrete countertops, bronze fixtures, and chef-worthy appliances. Ryker cooked the basics, but he'd appreciated the aesthetic of the kitchen when he bought the place. Large, black-framed windows and fourteen-foot ceilings gave the apartment an airy feel, and the exposed brick wall on the far side provided a warm contrast to the modern touches.

The blue velvet sectional and artwork were the few pops of color in the living space. The bedroom was at the back along with a den and a spacious spa bathroom, his one luxury. It was a small apartment by many standards, but it was his—a peaceful haven in which to live and write. He vividly remembered the day he'd signed the paperwork and gotten the keys. He wasn't much for showing his feelings, but even he had teared up. Coming from a childhood where food and shelter were inconsistent, Ryker was appreciative of everything he had worked hard for.

A loud meow interrupted his musings.

Isaac, one of Ryker's three fur babies, wandered over to complain to his human. Ryker had adopted the large white Persian cat from the rescue shelter downtown where he volunteered. Isaac's previous owner had noticed a flaw in one of the cat's copper-colored eyes, decided he would not be able to enter him in any competitions, and promptly left him at the shelter. That person's loss was Ryker's gain.

Isaac bounded into Ryker's lap and curled up in a tight ball, his ears flicking back and whiskers twitching to signal his displeasure that his human had yet to pay him any attention this morning.

"Okay, Isaac, sorry for neglecting you, but it's back to work for me soon."

Ryker murmured nonsense to Isaac while stroking his long, sleek back, and Ryker's body relaxed as the vibration from the purrs grew stronger. While Isaac welcomed Ryker's touch, the cat was not keen on others—neither Mac nor Cal could pet the beautiful beast without receiving a few scratches. They had taken to greeting the cat by name only and leaving well enough alone. His other cat, a black-and-white tabby named Princess Leia, usually stayed in her big bed, sound asleep. Spock was Ryker's third furry roommate, a miniature pinscher rescue with big ears and unlimited energy.

Ryker had a soft spot for animals of all kinds ever since he was a kid. He'd rescued everything from birds to cats and even a rat at one point. His mother hadn't been amused at the last one, however, and forbade him from any further rodent rescue operations. But that didn't stop his love for animals—it had only grown as he got older. Ryker had been dropping by the local animal shelter to volunteer for a few hours every week for the past decade. He'd also made several anonymous donations to ensure they could continue to rescue and re-home as many animals as possible.

He continued to pet Isaac and let his thoughts drift, thinking about the upcoming party. Ryker's lack of social skills—or lack of concern about them—was probably the reason he gravitated toward animals as well as writing. He didn't care much about people's expectations. He did what he enjoyed, and as long as he was honest with himself, he was good. All these thoughts made his body tense again. Isaac jumped off his lap and strutted to his climbing tower near the desk, mewling loudly.

Ryker shook himself out of his musings and opened up his laptop, Googling Wesley Stewart. Mac would have his arguments ready to persuade Ryker to work with this guy, so Ryker needed to prepare his rebuttal. He'd need more than just a "hell fucking no" response to this ridiculous collaboration idea.

Ryker scanned the numerous photographs of Wes online, some from events, others from social media posts, a few from his TV talk show appearances. He had to admit that Wes was a stunning man: tall and broad, with short, stylized blond hair, hazel eyes, and a spattering of freckles over a sharp nose. He had full lips and dimples when he smiled, which only amplified Wes's fierce beauty. Going through the pictures, Ryker noticed a tall man with curly brown hair standing near Wes at several events. Friend? Lover?

Lover?

"Why the fuck should I care about that?" Ryker said aloud. "Stop looking at the pretty man and get back to your research."

Ryker perused the Web, wanting to know what Wes himself had to say. There was a YouTube recording of an interview Wes had done five years ago, when his first self-help book was released. He was talkative and charming and had the host in stitches. Very smooth. Maybe too smooth. When the interviewer asked about a special person in his life, Wes laughed and said he enjoyed dating a variety of men. Well, he was open about his sexuality, no question. But then there was an ask about Wes's family, and another about whether he would return to writing fiction, and you could see the physical change in his posture and face. Wes's smile vanished and he deftly changed the subject. Interesting sore points. Ryker would file that away for future reference.

Writers were curious by nature, and Ryker was

interested in learning all about Wes and his motivations. He'd go along with Mac's plans for now. He'd listen and learn, and then make an informed decision. Or maybe he'd just shut the whole thing down.

Ryker printed out a picture of Wes and taped it to his board. He couldn't help but stare at it for a long, long time.

Chapter Two
Wes

Ahh, springtime in New York City. Wes loved it. He sat at a small table on the outdoor patio adjacent to his Park Avenue hotel, the wind ruffling his hair as he quietly sipped his second morning latte.

Locals and tourists were out and about, soaking up the May sunshine that had been absent over the long, bitter winter. Honking cars, rumbling motors, and crowds of people shuffling down the street all culminated in the energetic vibration that was New York City. Yup, the pulse of the city Wes loved, second only to his hometown of Toronto, was jumping today.

Wrapped in his navy Burberry trench coat, he took a moment to enjoy his break and people-watch before the busy day ahead. His phone buzzed with repeated notifications, jarring his cup and utensils on the table. Reluctantly, he glanced down at it. One missed call: Mac Duran.

While Wes was pleased at what he'd accomplished with his writing career to this point, including the attention of many fans who enjoyed his books, he'd started to feel more and more dissatisfied. Self-help books made him a household name, but he hardly ever had a moment to himself anymore. A big part of his job was endless media junkets and talking so much that names and faces and cities started to blur. He used to love the travel and attention, but not recently. Lately he found himself repeating the same conversations with different people, only touching the surface of things. No spark, no debate. He hadn't experienced a meaningful connection in a very long time. Writing still gave him some enjoyment, but it took more and more effort to focus on that, too, which worried him most of all.

When Mac Duran had called two weeks ago and suggested a meeting here in New York City to discuss a book series with R.D. Smith, Wes immediately said yes. The timing was perfect since Wes was in town for the start of his cross-country book tour. And while he was familiar with R.D.'s work, he didn't know anything about the author. For the first time in a long time, Wes was excited and motivated.

It's been five years since you wrote a mystery novel. Maybe you don't have it in you anymore. Would he be able to get back in the groove, just like that? He still wasn't sure. But Mac's phone call was a gift Wes wouldn't refuse, and he was hopeful that working with another author would help get him back to the writing he once loved. The only thing he loved.

At thirty-six, Wes lived alone. Just the way he liked it. His last relationship with Kieran—if he could call it a relationship—had lasted only a couple of months. This was back when he was thirty-three and riding high on his newfound self-help success. Kieran had shown his true nature by trying to sell Wes's private details to the tabloids, and that was the end of things. Wes went back to casual fucks. No personal revelations required, no hurt feelings, no feelings period. Attraction, action, out the bathroom or hotel door, the end. Next. No way was he going to be that vulnerable ever again. People only wanted the successful persona anyway and became infatuated with the celebrity lifestyle. They didn't care about him personally, his dreams, his fears. No, anything deep and meaningful, he experienced through his writing, and that alone sustained him. Or at least, it used to.

His inner musings were interrupted by an incoming call from Luca. He'd been Wes's loyal assistant for the past eight years and was one of the few people

Wes considered a close friend.

Trustworthy, kind, and terrifyingly organized, Luca Santino had a bold personality and a personal style to match. Luca had a quick answer for everything and wasn't afraid to give Wes his honest, if somewhat saucy, opinion. Wes was pretty laid back about most things in life—why stress when it solved nothing? Luca, on the other hand, seemed to thrive on chaos and took great pride in tackling the most challenging situations. Luca had recently launched his event-planning business on the side, and Wes knew that it was only a matter of time before he left his employ for good.

"Good morning, Luca. Yes, I arrived safely in the Big Apple, just like I texted you last night, and yes, I am on my way to meet Mac shortly," he said while continuing to sip his coffee.

"I know that, Wesley. I have a tracker on your phone." Luca chuckled. "Kidding! Anyhoo, I was calling to remind you that Greyson flew down this morning and will meet you at Mac's office at eleven AM. He also changed his mind and will accompany you to the dinner party at eight PM tomorrow." Luca paused, and Wes could hear typing, as well as what sounded like Luca's favorite singer, Adele, in the background. "Your interview tomorrow over the lunch hour at Storico has been moved from one to one thirty PM, and a different reporter will attend. I've forwarded her bio to you and Greyson."

Greyson Ineja was Wes's PR rep and oldest friend. Grey built and ran a successful national public relations business based in Toronto. Most of the day-to-day client dealings were taken care of by his staff, but Grey still handled a few high profile clients like Wes as a personal favor. Grey kept himself occupied with work twenty-four seven since his wife, Andrea, passed away over a year ago in a car accident. Wes had encouraged Grey to take time off, but he refused. Wes often wondered if Grey's marriage had been worth the pain he now saw in his friend's eyes. Grey had assured Wes that one day he would understand. Wes still wasn't convinced.

"Grey texted me a few minutes ago. Thanks for the updated reporter bio. Anything else I need to know? Have you reorganized my closet again? My kitchen? Don't forget, the bedroom is a no-go zone after last time." Wes laughed. Luca openly acknowledged his hyper-organized tendencies, but after Wes had discovered his bedroom drawer of sex supplies and toys neatly labeled and arranged, the nightstand was deemed off limits.

"You laugh, but I'm sure you appreciate finding what you need quickly when the mood strikes. Anyway, getting back to actual work, I also confirmed the timing for your appearance on *Weekend New York* on Sunday. Oh, and I packed you lots of condoms and lube. Play safe." Luca snorted and hung up.

Wes chuckled and glanced around at the other tables, taking note of various couples and singles chatting away, listening to music, or working. He signaled the waiter for his bill, and once he was all settled up, he grabbed his phone and laptop. He decided to walk to Mac's office, given the mild weather.

As he rose to his full six-foot-one height, his eyes caught on a handsome brunet man in a navy striped suit at the far end of the patio. The man smiled at Wes, staring for a very long time. Then the man gestured at him to come over. As Wes approached, the man stood up and nodded, the lust evident in his big brown eyes.

"I couldn't help but notice you sitting there by yourself. You're much too handsome to be without company. Would you like to join me? I'm Duncan," the man murmured, smiling flirtatiously and placing his hand on Wes's arm. His warm eyes and wide smile were definitely appealing, but Wes just wasn't in the mood for a hook-up, nor did he have time today.

"You're too kind, Duncan, but unfortunately, I have a busy day ahead," he replied with his practiced grin. "Enjoy the sunshine."

And with that, Wes went on his way. He could feel the man staring at his back, or more likely his ass, and for a moment, he thought about returning to get his number. He let that idea drift away. Maybe tomorrow night, after the dinner party, he could find a club and a sexy man to spend a few pleasurable hours with. He'd get rid of his stress and clear his head for the upcoming week.

Right now, he needed to focus on work and get his in-demand ass moving. Walking briskly, he was thankful that his morning runs had paid off. He arrived on time without breaking much of a sweat.

Entering the art deco building on Fifth Avenue, he couldn't help but appreciate the large windows and stark, geometric design. He looked around the lobby and spotted Grey sitting in a black leather chair, checking his phone with one hand and running the other through his curly chestnut hair, which now had quite a few grey strands. Wes teased Grey that he was finally starting to live up to his namesake. He also noticed the lines of tension around Grey's mouth and the prominent cheekbones that seemed sharper than ever. He reminded himself to be extra attentive to his friend and ensure Grey enjoyed himself while on this business trip.

"Hey, lazy ass, ready to get this week underway?" Wes yelled out as he approached with a wave. He noted Grey's half smile, and when his friend came over, Wes leaned down and gave him a hug. Grey was a few inches shorter than Wes, with a slimmer build that was bordering on skinny lately. Grey lingered in the hug, and Wes gave one final squeeze to comfort his friend before he let go.

"I've never been lazy a day in my life, you fucker!" Grey said jokingly as he smacked Wes's shoulder. "I have a good feeling about this meeting, Wes. I'm excited to see what Mac has to say." They walked together to the elevator in the center of the lobby. "What about the rest of the week? Any concerns about your public appearances? The interview tomorrow or the show Sunday?" That was Grey, right back to business. He was a problem-solver by nature: calm, cool, and way too collected.

Wes smiled at his friend and shook his head. "Everything will be fine, Grey. My only concern is this potential book deal. It's an intriguing carrot that Mac's dangling under my nose, and I'm ready to bite."

The elevator pinged loudly when they arrived at the twenty-fifth floor, and they entered a sleek office with a wall of posters that Wes recognized as best-selling book covers. Lots of white leather furniture and colorful artwork filled the space. A smiling receptionist sat at a glossy desk, her fuchsia pixie cut and matching lips a sharp complement to the cool decor. "Good morning and welcome to Duran Communications. How can I assist you?" she asked as her big blue eyes roved slowly over both men.

"Good morning. Wes Stewart and Greyson Ineja to see Mac Duran," Grey smoothly replied, sliding his business card across the desktop along with a returning, albeit cooler, smile.

"Of course. Can I offer you a beverage while you're waiting? Latte? Vitamin Water? My name is

Helena, by the way," she said.

"Just spring water for the two of us, please and thanks, Helena," Wes said with his trademark grin, noting her sigh as she walked off behind her desk.

Grey turned to him and rolled his eyes. "Guess she doesn't read the tabloids and all your adventures with men. Many, many men," he joked.

Before Wes could provide a smart-ass comeback, the door at the end of the hallway opened and Mac appeared, walking toward them. The dark expression on his sharp face was so intense that he seemed to suck all the air from the room. But as he came closer, his icy countenance morphed into a huge grin. "How the fuck did you two jokers get past building security?" he asked.

"Mac, great to see you again." Wes held out his hand. Mac grabbed it and gave him a quick hug—just a friendly one. Wes didn't feel any spark of attraction to Mac, and he preferred it that way. Separation of business and pleasure was usually best.

Usually.

"So glad you're here, Wes." Mac smiled and turned to Grey to shake his hand. "Grey, it's been a long time." He paused and his smile faded. "I'm sorry again about Andrea. How have you been?"

Wes heard Grey's quick intake of breath and looked over to see if his friend needed support.

"I'm taking it day by day," Grey said, then gave a quick smile and pointed at Wes. "It helps to have good friends like this charming ass here." Wes chuckled. "How about you, Mac? Business good?" Grey asked, deftly changing the subject.

"It's been a good year. I have other businesses under my global communications brand, but the publishing arm is special to me. My grandfather started it, so I want to keep it going as long as possible. But who knows—the publishing world gets smaller and smaller every year. Anyway, let's head on back to my office."

Mac led them down the hallway and into a large corner office with minimal furniture and plenty of natural light. He gestured to two sleek chairs in front of the desk. There was a knock at the door and Helena entered, sliding the glasses of water onto the desk, then silently leaving.

Wes looked around, noticing several pictures on the wall behind Mac, including many famous authors, celebrities, and artists. No pictures on his desk, though. No personal touches. Wes didn't know much about Mac except that he was a workaholic, had wicked negotiating skills, and was very well connected in this city. At his last visit, Wes and Mac had chatted about the best restaurants and clubs to visit, but there was no talk of a boyfriend, partner, or family, except for Mac's grandfather. Wes was always curious about people and their stories, but decided to put his nosy inclinations about Mac aside for the time being.

Mac leaned forward, his forearms on his desk, and his cool green eyes assessed them. "Are we ready to talk about a potential new book series?" he asked, pointing to his laptop. "I've drafted a sample proposal for a three-book deal, as well as timelines and the prospective offer for you to review with Grey. Keep in mind, this is a draft for your review only at the moment. R.D. has yet to provide his buy-in. And I want to warn you, this will be a demanding project. That said, I think it means good things for your respective careers. I've invited R.D. to dinner Saturday so you can meet in a more relaxed environment. I mentioned the collaboration, but he still isn't sold on the idea, so don't be offended if he seems unreceptive." Mac gave a small sigh, a slight grimace on his face.

"What?" Wes blurted out in shock. "Why isn't he sold on the idea?" In past, he was the one who rejected requests from others for work collaborations. What the fuck?

Mac shrugged. "All I can say is R.D. prefers to work solo. If you want more details, you'll have to ask him directly. Taking on a writing partner is a big deal, and you'll need to ensure you're a good match. I'm going on my instinct and experience and based on both your work and your personalities. I think there's some interesting contrasts that will play out very nicely."

Wes pondered Mac's input, and his curiosity over this book deal—and now R.D. Smith—grew stronger. Wes was used to getting what he wanted, and this would be no different. No way would he allow Mr. Reluctant to write him off (pun intended) before they'd talked it out.

"Well, it looks like this could be a far more interesting venture than I expected. There's nothing I like better than using my charm to convince unreceptive audiences to do my bidding." He smirked. Mac sighed and Grey rolled his eyes.

"I thought Canadians were humble," Mac said as he pointed at Wes.

"Wes defies stereotypes," Grey responded wryly, then turned to Wes. "Someday, Wes, that arrogance is going to come back and bite you in the ass."

Wes's grin grew bigger. "My ass looks forward to it," he replied. All three men broke out into laughter.

Mac and Grey continued to chat about Wes's upcoming book tour while Wes thought about this new project. He was confident that by this time next week, he would have a new book deal and a new writing partner.

Convince R.D. to work with him? The deal was as good   as   signed.

Chapter Three
Ryker

Ryker was running as fast as he could.

He couldn't see his attacker, but he could hear their heavy breathing and pounding footsteps behind him. Suddenly, a large hand grabbed his arm. Ryker couldn't get loose—he was caught, trapped—

No, not again, let go! Stop!

He opened his eyes to find his dog, Spock, by the side of his bed, his wet nose nuzzling Ryker's palm. *It's okay. I'm okay,* he said to himself. It was just another nightmare.

Would he ever stop having them? How many years would it take?

These thoughts sent his body into a total spiral. Sweat covered his skin. His heart pounded. His ears filled with a high-pitched buzzing noise, and his airway felt constricted. Pain radiated from his chest into his back. He reared up out of his king-sized bed, threw off the navy duvet, and turned on the bedside lamp, reaching for his glasses. He glanced at his phone: two forty-six AM.

Get up. Get up, he repeated to himself. *Get moving. It's not a heart attack. It's just anxiety. Move. Don't think, move.*

Throwing on black lounge pants, he rushed into his living room and turned on every light, his fear slowly ebbing. He made his way over to the large oak desk by the window, the one that looked out over Central Park, and logged onto his laptop. Spock quietly followed him and lay down on top of his feet, offering comfort to his human.

Ryker then did the only thing that kept him sane and grounded no matter what happened in his life—he wrote.

In the middle of the night, it didn't really matter if the words were novel-worthy. Getting lost in his imagination helped exorcise his thoughts. Invested in his characters and their stories, he forgot about his own problems for a little while.

He stopped momentarily and rubbed the lava rock bracelets on his left wrist, counting each bead to distract his mind and bring his heart back to a normal rhythm. People often told him the bracelets were a cool fashion statement, and he didn't care to correct them. Counting items was one of several coping mechanisms Ryker had learned during therapy to help bring calm. Anything to bring calm.

A short while later, he could feel his body slowly normalizing, his heart rate now at an easy pace and his breathing slower and deeper. Ryker continued to work, getting lost in his creativity, letting the story take him wherever it needed to go. Time passed quickly when he got caught up in his writing, and when he next glanced at his phone, it was four thirty-four AM.

"Okay, Spock, time to close up shop and try to go back to sleep." He closed his laptop and motioned to his dog, and they sauntered off down the hallway. Snuggling back under the covers in his bed, Ryker rubbed his tired eyes and turned on his sleep app. Twenty minutes later, the room was filled with human snores and animal rumbles.

****

It seemed like he had fallen asleep only a second ago when the sound of his phone ringing woke him at eleven AM. Cal.

Mac, Cal, and Ryker had been friends for almost two decades. Ryker was the moody introvert, Mac the persuasive dealmaker, and Cal was the life of the party.

He was a successful artist and one of the kindest people Ryker had ever met, and his unfiltered mouth was hilarious and sometimes frightening in its honesty. You were always in for an interesting time with Cal.

"Hey, trouble. What's up?" Ryker asked in his sleepy voice.

"My dick, for a good four hours. Man, those erectile medications aren't kidding! 'Don't take more than the recommended dose'—good advice for you, my friend. Thought I'd have to head over to the ER if I didn't calm down soon." He laughed.

Ryker rolled his eyes and sat up in bed. "Very funny, like you need sex meds. So, what's going on? How are you?"

"I'm good. Busy finishing up a commissioned piece, then I have another one to get started. And I'll be working on a new series for the exhibit in December. Other than that, the usual antics. A hot man here, a gorgeous woman there, a threesome if they ask nicely. Oh, and I'm looking forward to Mac's party Saturday night. Hopefully, there'll be some pretty people for me to have some sexy fun with." Cal paused, and the lighthearted tone of his voice suddenly changed. "Anyway, besides saying hi, there was a specific reason that I called you."

"Sure, what's on your mind?"

"Hmm, so," Cal continued, "I've received these text messages over the past month that are kinda creepy, and I wanted your opinion."

"What do you mean?" Ryker asked, his body tensing. "Creepy as in weird texts from someone you know, or creepy from an unknown number?"

Cal paused before he answered. "The latter. The messages tell me that I'm behaving like a whore. I'm cheating on 'my soulmate,' and I should be punished for my sins. Shit like that. It's crazy talk, obviously, given that I'm not married or in a relationship and the very idea of having a soulmate gives me a rash. I thought the first one was a sick joke. I blocked the number, but similar messages keep appearing from two different numbers. They all repeat the same story: I'm cheating and I'm going to be punished. I assume this is just a weird joke, but I'm getting a bit freaked out. What should I do, Ry?"

Ryker's short stint covering the crime beat in New York City had led him to several horrible scenes he would rather forget, but it had also given him insight and made him particularly aware of personal safety.

"Things like this can escalate quickly if you don't take them seriously," he said. "If you receive another weird text, tempted as you may be to delete it, don't. A phone call from an unknown number, record it. If a physical threat is made, go to the police. Log everything." Ryker paused. "And make sure the security settings on your devices and at your home are updated. Don't treat this as a prank until it's proven otherwise. It could be a sick joke, and let's hope it's just that, but you need to be proactive."

Ryker heard Cal's sudden intake of breath on the other end of the line and sought to reassure his friend.

"Hey, Mac and I are here, and we'd do anything for you. You know that, right? Just keep us in the loop." Ryker got up and stared out his window. "Maybe you can join me at my Krav Maga class on Friday. It never hurts to brush up on self-defense in this city."

"Thanks, Ry, I appreciate your advice. I hope I didn't upset you, but I didn't know who else to ask, and I didn't want to tell Mac. Not yet. You know how protective he gets. I'm sure it's just a prank, but the last text kinda freaked me out a bit."

Cal was such a happy, carefree person so for him

to admit he was scared was something.

"You can tell me anything. You know that," Ryker said. "Say, do you want to meet up for lunch or something?"

"Thanks, but I'm not leaving my place until I finish this piece, and then I have to contact the gallery. Let's share a ride to Mac's tomorrow, okay? I'll arrange it and text you the info in the aft."

"Sounds good. You sure you're okay?" Ryker asked again.

"I'm fine, bud. I feel better now that we've talked. Later, gator." Cal ended the call on a lighter note.

Ryker sent a quick text to Mac, letting him know they needed to talk privately Saturday night. His nervousness about the party vanished, replaced with a very deep and real concern over Cal's safety. He hoped the texts were a prank, but Ryker didn't want Cal to take any chances.

Ryker's phone buzzed with notifications from his editor, and he focused on work, pushing everything else out of his mind. Writing kept him grounded, no matter what.

He tried to imagine what a partner might do to his routine, and he didn't like it. Not one bit.

Chapter Four
Wes

New grey herringbone suit—check.

Hair styled, fresh shave, breath mints—triple check.

Condoms and lube—here's hoping.

Saturday night had finally arrived. After two days of meetings and interviews about his latest book, Wes was ready to enjoy some good food, lively conversation, and maybe some dancing and other physical pursuits later on. He glanced at his reflection in the bathroom mirror, noting the circles under his hazel eyes. He was having trouble sleeping again, despite the success of the last few days.

Doing his best to ignore the issue, he checked his e-mail and opened up the document Luca had sent him. Not much to tell about R.D. Smith, except what was posted on his social media pages, which was likely controlled by his PR machine. Obviously, the author liked his privacy. Wes would be meeting the man in person tonight, anyway, and he would draw his own conclusions about this potential partnership. Wes smiled, remembering Mac's warning that Wes would need to sell himself. Well, he was really fucking good at that. He texted Grey to let him know he'd be down in the lobby bar.

Half an hour later, Wes was sipping vodka on ice and enjoying a live jazz trio at the bar when Grey walked in and sat down on the brown leather stool beside him.

"Gin and tonic with lime, please," Grey murmured to the smiling female bartender, fiddling with the napkin placed in front of him. "So, all set for tonight, Wes? Got your pitch ready?"

"I don't need to get ready. I'm just going to be my amazing self and get what I want, as always," Wes replied with a huge smirk and a raise of his glass.

Grey laughed and rolled his eyes. "I really wish you had more self-confidence, Wes." The bartender came back with Grey's drink, and Grey nodded his thanks. "I think one of these days, you're going to meet someone who won't be swayed by your charm and give you whatever you want. I just hope I'm there to see it." He mirrored Wes's actions and raised his drink. They both chuckled and clinked glasses. They sipped on their drinks quietly for a moment until Wes broke the silence.

"How are you really holding up, Grey? You seem tired. Are you eating and sleeping okay?" Wes remarked.

"I won't lie. Losing Andrea has been the most difficult thing I've ever endured." Grey paused and took another sip of his drink. "But I feel like I've finally turned a corner. At least I sleep more than three hours a night, and work keeps me busy. I'm just a little bit uncomfortable about socializing. I've met a few interesting people at my tennis club, and one asked me out on a date recently, but I turned them down. I don't know if I'm ready yet."

"Look, I can't imagine what you're going through, but at some point, you have to face your fear. It will be less painful when you're totally honest with people and they understand your situation."

"It's not just socializing." Grey looked around the room quickly and turned back to Wes, lowering his voice to a whisper. "I haven't had sex in so long, I feel fucking awkward. My body is telling me it's ready, but my mind is freaking out."

Ah, sex. One of Wes's favorite topics and pastimes. He looked at Grey directly. "You just need to get into an environment where you can relax. Maybe a club or a bar. Have a drink or two. Flirt a bit. Sex is one thing; dating is a whole other issue. Personally, I prefer the former. It's simpler and the variety is so enjoyable."

"Easy for you to say. You weren't married for eight years. I haven't had sex with more than one person in all that time. Now I feel like a dorky teenager again." Grey chuckled quietly and shook his head.

"Less thinking and more doing, and you'll be all set."

They finished their drinks and left the bar to catch their car service. Wes's stomach suddenly tightened—with trepidation or excitement, he couldn't tell, but it had been a long time since he'd felt either.

He welcomed the feeling, embraced it, and smiled to himself as they headed off into the vibrant New York City night.

****

Ryker

"So, what do you think?"

Ryker stood in front of the full-length mirror in his walk-in closet and looked down expectantly at his three fur babies, all of whom had watched his every move as he got ready over the past half hour. He'd chosen slim black designer jeans, a charcoal t-shirt, and a black velvet blazer. He'd added a lava bead necklace and left his dark hair loose. In addition to his usual bracelets, he'd strapped a leather cuff to his right wrist. He decided to forego glasses tonight in favor of contacts and added navy eyeliner to complete his look. He mulled a quick shave, but decided the scruff was better. Combined with the dark eyeliner, it made him look edgier and unapproachable. Perfect.

He slipped into his old combat boots and grabbed his phone, noticing that Cal had texted him a few minutes ago.

Cal: **Got our ride ready. Move your ass!**

Impatient, as usual. Ryker shook his head and hurried down the hallway to the front door.

Thankfully, the elevator ride was a short one, and when he got to the spacious lobby of his building, his gaze immediately caught on the limo out front. Jesus, it was a bit much for a short ride to a dinner party. But who was he to argue with Cal's over-the-top style or generosity? The man was outgoing, funny, and flirtatious to the max—a platinum blond, brown-eyed imp with a personality no one could resist. Even grumpy-ass Ryker.

The back window rolled down to reveal Cal's blond hair and big smile. Ryker opened the door and glanced in at his friend, who had a glass of bubbly in hand.

"Really? You're dressed like *that* for a dinner party?" Ryker exclaimed.

Cal was relaxed in a slim white tuxedo jacket and pants but no shirt. As he stretched his arms out over the back of the leather seats, the jacket opened to display his chest and gold nipple piercings. Cal liked to push the fashion envelope and hated restrictive clothing and clothing in general.

"Jesus, Cal, why didn't you put a shirt on! Save that outfit for the clubs." Ryker was half amused, half horrified at Cal's clothing choice.

"Come on, Ry, I look hot." Cal winked at Ryker and smoothed his hands through his chin-length hair, then down his jacket lapels. "Besides, this way all the attention will fall on me, and you'll be left in peace, just like you prefer. Or at least, that was my plan until you wrecked it with the eyeliner. People are going to stare, bud. You look pretty hot yourself."

Ryker grunted, squirming uncomfortably at that

comment. "This look is supposed to repel people, not attract them. Aren't you getting my 'fuck off' vibe?"

"No, I'm getting 'I'm down to fuck' more than 'fuck off.' Bad boys are irresistible, didn't you know?" Cal's teasing laughter filled the limo.

"I'm grumpy, not bad." Ryker pouted, then accepted the glass of champagne Cal held out to him, forcing himself to relax. "And how come you're so happy? Have the text messages stopped?"

"Nothing today, so that's good. Anyway, I don't want to think about it tonight. We both need to de-stress and have fun." Ryker accepted Cal's point and refrained from any further questions.

Cal chatted away about his day, and Ryker rolled the window down to watch Manhattan whiz by. Soon, they were in front of Mac's three-story brownstone in the East Village.

Cal got out first and walked nonchalantly up the stairs, ignoring several passersby on the sidewalk as they gaped at his outfit—or lack thereof.

Mac opened his front door, dressed in trim navy slacks and a white button-down, his practiced smile in place until he looked down at Cal's outfit.

"I didn't order a stripper. You have the wrong address." Mac managed to get halfway through his comment with a straight face, and then he and Ryker bent over snickering, their laughter echoing in the cool night air.

"Hey, I'm fucking sexy and I know it." Cal smirked as he opened his arms wide and gestured down his body. "And you should be used to this by now. Wearing the least amount of clothing necessary is my trademark."

"You're ridiculous is what you are. But we love you anyway," Ryker muttered, shaking his head.

Mac ushered them through the door and into his modern foyer. Ryker watched as his two closest friends embraced, big grins on both their faces.

"Mac, you didn't tell me it would be *that* kind of party," a deep voice boomed from behind them, and they all turned to look at the man who had spoken.

Fuck me, Ryker thought as he got a good look at the tall, gorgeous man who stood casually at the end of the hallway with his hands in the pockets of his dark grey dress pants. In the dim light of the chandelier, Ryker could make out the man's thick blond hair, styled in an undercut, sharp cheekbones, and light eyes.

Fucking hell, this was Wes Stewart. Ryker recognized him from his social media. Ryker couldn't control the look of surprise on his face or the jolt of anger that rippled through his body at this unwelcome surprise. He hadn't known he'd be meeting Wes tonight, and he wasn't prepared. And the pretentious prick had a smug grin on his face that meant he was all too aware that he had the advantage. *Yeah, we'll see about that.* Ryker clenched his fists. Mac had a lot of explaining to do.

"Sorry, those parties take place on Thursday nights," Mac replied sardonically as he ushered Cal and Ryker down the hallway to make introductions. "Wes, I'd like you to meet my two best friends." He paused, glanced at Cal's chest, and shook his head. "The half-dressed one is Callum Pattison, one of New York's most successful artists and illustrators." He turned to his left. "And the man in black here is Ryker Desoumas."

Now that he was getting a good look up close, Ryker could see that Wes's eyes were a luminous hazel, a unique combination of green and gold, surrounded by thick, dark blond lashes and fine laugh lines that crinkled when he smiled. Freckles dotted his nose and cheekbones. A square jawline and dimples drew Ryker's eye directly to Wes's heart-shaped lips—a sexy contrast to his masculine profile. He also smelled amazing, fresh and warm, like a sun-kissed afternoon by the sea.

After greeting Cal, Wes turned his attention to Ryker and extended his hand, those amazing eyes boring right into him. Ryker's palm met Wes's strong, warm grip and the touch sparked off a chain reaction; his whole body flushed and his cock twitched. He'd never been so affected by a simple handshake. *Snap out of it,* he admonished himself.

"Ryker is otherwise known as R.D. Smith, the often grumpy but much loved and very talented author."

Mac's mention of his pen name edged Ryker out of his hormonal trance. He glared at Wes, who returned the look with a huge smile, including a big dimple in his left cheek. Smug, handsome bastard. What was so amusing, and what exactly had Mac told Wes?

Before Ryker could issue a sarcastic comment, a tall, slim man with curly brown hair stepped into the foyer beside Wes and reached out his hand. Ryker recognized him from his online research.

"Greyson Ineja. I'm Wes's oldest friend and his long-suffering PR lackey," he said with a warm, genuine smile.

Ryker noticed that Cal was suddenly quiet, standing there staring at Greyson's face, which was totally unlike his friend. He nudged Cal with his elbow, and finally, Cal awakened from whatever daydream he was lost in and was back to his usual flirty self.

"It's so very nice to meet you, Wes and Greyson." Cal gave his biggest smile to Grey, along with a thorough once-over. "Greyson. Mmm, your name is so sexy. It really suits you."

Greyson's face reddened at the compliment. "It's nice to meet you all. I need to get back to the party and mingle with the other guests." And with that, Greyson abruptly turned and headed back into Mac's living room.

The hallway was silent for a few moments before Wes explained, "Grey lost his wife just over a year ago. He's a bit out of practice when it comes to flirting."

"Shit, I'm sorry, Wes." Cal's face flushed, and he ran his hands through his hair. "I hope I didn't offend him. I'll go apologize."

"No worries, he'll be okay. Grey dated men and women before he got married, so getting hit on is nothing new. Go and have a chat with him. You'll see, he's fine."

"Good idea. Come on, Cal, I'm neglecting my other guests." Mac grabbed Cal's arm as they headed off, and suddenly, Ryker found himself alone in the hallway with Wes.

Shit.

Chapter Five
Wes

Shit.

Wes hadn't known what to expect when he met R.D. Smith—Ryker—but it certainly wasn't the man standing in front of him. Arousal had coursed through his blood as soon as their eyes met, and when their hands touched, holy shit, it felt like his palm had been scorched by fire.

Ryker. He loved that name. It suited this dark angel.

Angel? What the fuck? Am I a poet all of a sudden?

But for some reason, those words seemed to fit. Then again, the incredibly hot and seemingly irritated man before him could be mistaken for a moody rockstar with long black hair, facial scruff, and sleek black clothing that clung to his lean body. The provocative eyeliner was the icing on the cake, drawing Wes into the most beautiful deep blue eyes he'd ever seen. Unfortunately, those eyes were swirling with anger. At him. Ryker was absently rubbing the bracelets on his wrist and glaring at Wes like he was the devil himself. Well, maybe Wes would need to be if he wanted this book deal to happen. If Ryker was a dark angel in this scenario, then Wes was a cheeky devil, light and playful but determined to get what he wanted. Too bad Wes's body had reacted so viscerally to Ryker when they had to stick to being professionals. For the time being.

"It's a pleasure to meet you in person at last, Ryker. I've read and enjoyed your books, and I hope we can have a chat about Mac's idea and see where it takes us. Why don't we join the others and get to know each other?" Wes said smoothly, gesturing to the living room.

Before Ryker could reply, Wes turned, and Ryker followed closely behind. Wes slowed his steps deliberately, allowing him to feel Ryker's body heat as they walked through the doorway, and a warm, spicy scent surrounded him. Fuck, Ryker smelled amazing, like leather and cinnamon.

Stop. Focus on the deal, not your dick, he reminded himself.

Wes snagged two glasses of champagne from the bar at the far end of the living room and took a moment to admire Mac's spacious, modern home. The room was filled with large, low furniture in earth tones and sparse wood accents, as well as colorful art, which resulted in a relaxed, elegant vibe. Twenty or so guests occupied the space, filling it with conversational murmurs, occasional laughter, and the clink of glassware. Wes turned to hand a glass to Ryker and was greeted by that penetrating blue glare again.

"Ryker, you're going to age that pretty face of yours frowning at me like that. Here, sip on this and let's find a quiet corner to talk," he murmured, offering up his best smile.

"No need for compliments or quiet corners, Wes. I'll get right to the point. I work alone. That's it. I know Mac means well, but I enjoy my working life the way it is. It's nothing personal. I just don't need a writing partner. I'm sorry if this has been a waste of your time, but I told Mac it wasn't a good idea at the outset. But, like the stubborn man he is, he's going to keep trying to convince me. As, I'm sure, will you. Good luck with that."

Ryker raised his champagne glass in a mock toast and headed off to the other side of the room. Wes didn't have a difficult time with witty comebacks, but in that moment, he had nothing.

Wes stared at Ryker as he walked away, his eyes inevitably straying lower to get a good, long look at his ass, modeled perfectly in tight denim. He shook his head to get his mind off his reaction and wake up the rational part of his brain.

Ryker thought he'd had the last word, but Wes wasn't going to let a little excuse like "I work alone" deter him. He had a gut feeling about this book series, and now that he'd met Ryker and experienced their initial chemistry, it would only make this project that much more exciting and interesting.

Wes didn't need luck. He just had to be patient.

****

Ryker

Twenty minutes later, palms sweating, Ryker forced a polite smile as he pretended to listen to the conversation going on around him at the dinner table. Wes kept glancing over from the opposite end, that dimpled grin on his face. *What the hell is that guy so fucking happy about?* Ryker had said no. Did Wes think he was going to change his mind? The sexy asshole was just trying to play with his head. His dick twitched in his jeans at that thought.

No, not that head. Calm down, he told his dick. *Wes is the enemy.*

His dick did not agree.

Ryker watched as Wes turned his attention back to Mac, and suddenly, they bent their heads together and lowered their voices in what looked like an intense conversation. Unfortunately, Ryker was too far away to hear what they were saying. Besides which, Cal was going on about one of his crazy adventures, and the resulting laughter that filled the room blotted out any other conversations.

"And then I was buck-ass naked in the middle of the fucking piazza at two in the morning, being chased by a really angry husband and a horde of Italian police." Peals of laughter echoed in the large dining space.

Shaking out of his internal angst, Ryker looked across the table and noticed that Grey was paying particular attention to Cal's animated face—and flushing every time Cal said something flirtatious or outrageous. *Interesting.*

A large hand suddenly landed on Ryker's left thigh and squeezed tight. *Oh, no. Harrison Ruehl.*

Harrison was a successful fashion entrepreneur, a very wealthy businessman, and a regular at these parties. An admitted sugar daddy, Harrison kept trying to convince Ryker to "play" with him and be his boy, despite Ryker's insistence that he was not interested in that role. Ryker put on his fake smile, which was more like a grimace, and quietly removed the offending hand. Harrison didn't get the hint and gently touched Ryker's shoulder and hair. *Guess I'm not the only one who can't read social cues.*

"I was hoping to sit near you tonight and I lucked out. I figured I would finally be able to convince you to go out with me," Harrison purred as he leaned in. "I love your quiet nature. It's mysterious, and it intrigues me."

Rolling his eyes at Harrison's horrible attempt at a pick-up line, Ryker leaned away as far as he could. "Please don't touch my hair or any part of me. I've already told you that you and I are never going on a date. We want different things. You have a room full of other options," Ryker grumbled. He did his best to keep his voice low to avoid the attention of other guests, but he wasn't above making a scene if push came to shove. Some people needed to learn their lessons the hard way.

"But surely you need someone to help guide you and unleash your inner fire. I'd be happy to teach you," he said and slipped a business card into Ryker's jacket pocket.

Ryker took a deep breath and gave his best glare. "If you don't stop touching me in the next ten seconds, I will make a very loud comment about your inability to perform sexually."

"You wouldn't," Harrison scoffed.

"Try me," Ryker replied angrily. Harrison slowly withdrew his hand and shrugged.

Ryker breathed a big sigh of relief until a few minutes later, when Harrison once again placed his hand on Ryker's leg under the table.

It was going to be a long-ass night.

****

Wes

Who is that man practically sitting in Ryker's lap? Wes grumbled to himself as his mood took a distinct nosedive.

The large man to Ryker's left was probably in his fifties, with a shaved head and several visible tattoos. He was talking loudly and kept leaning into Ryker's personal space, touching his hair and shoulder. Ryker looked uncomfortable and pissed, even more so than when he was introduced to Wes, if that were possible. Or maybe that was his permanent expression. Words were exchanged and Wes observed the older man back off, and then his left hand moved under the table again. Wes felt the sudden urge to walk over and physically remove the man from his chair. *If that guy touches Ryker one more time...* White-hot anger burst through his blood, and it was all kinds of strange, because Wes was never possessive about anyone, let alone someone he had just met. *Control yourself, Wes, and focus.*

"How did your conversation with Ryker go?" Mac asked quietly, interrupting Wes's primal thoughts.

Wes turned his attention back to Mac and gave a small grin, trying to regain his calm. "He gave me the 'I work alone' speech and walked off. But I'm not that easy to get rid of. And I want answers. So, that being said, I need you to tell me a bit more about Ryker. Why's he refusing this collaboration before we even get a chance to talk it out? There must be a reason, and I'm not leaving New York before I know why." He paused and crossed his arms. "I mean it. I'm pigheaded that way. Ask my best friend." He pointed his thumb in Grey's direction.

Mac laughed softly, causing a dramatic change in his face. The savvy dealmaker was normally intense and almost grim-faced when he was in work mode, but when he relaxed, he was rather striking. Too bad Wes didn't feel a thing for Mac. Nope, it seemed his body and mind would rather focus on the hot, moody writer at the other end of the table.

"Ryker has his reasons for being hesitant," Mac said. "He was a journalist before becoming an author, and he left that job for a very good reason." Mac paused, steepling his hands, his expression once again intense. "I'll let him tell you his story in his own words. For now, let's just say that some scars run deep. Aside from that, Ryker is quiet, thoughtful, extremely smart. You'll notice that he prefers to have a few meaningful conversations rather than talk with everyone in a room. He hates publicity and attention. Expects and respects honesty and hard work. But he prefers to work on his own—be on his own, for the most part. I thought this collaboration would be good for him, push him out of his comfort zone a bit. Even great writers can get stuck in a rut, and he's headed into one. He has so much talent, but he needs a change.

Anyway, despite his attitude toward you, he is a good-hearted guy. Always supportive of his friends, me and Cal especially, no matter what crazy ideas we come up with," Mac finished and looked at Wes.

"Good information to know," Wes replied thoughtfully, contemplating his next move.

Mac's comment about meaningful conversations gave Wes an idea about how he might change Ryker's mind. In the meantime, he had other, more basic priorities.

He smiled at Mac. "So, any new clubs worth visiting while I'm in town? I'm ready to let loose."

Chapter Six
Ryker

After what seemed like a five-hour marathon dinner, Ryker excused himself to grab a smoke on Mac's rooftop patio. He didn't smoke often; he just liked the excuse to slip out for some much-needed space and quiet. All the loud conversations gave him a headache and drained his energy. He heard footsteps behind him and turned to see Mac approaching.

"Ry, you okay?" Mac asked.

"Yup, grabbing a smoke. You know the drill." He smiled, took a deep breath of the cool night air, and lit his cigarette. Suddenly, his chat with Cal earlier in the day resurfaced. "Hey, now that we have a moment to ourselves, I wanted to talk to you about Cal." He paused and pointed between them. "Keep this between us for now, okay? And don't freak out."

"All right, what's going on?" Mac asked intently.

Ryker paused again and took a drag on his cigarette, then slowly blew it out. "He's been receiving some strange texts lately from unknown numbers. I told him not to delete anything, to check his security settings, and go to the police if the situation escalates."

"What do you mean by strange?"

Ryker ran a hand through his hair. "They accuse Cal of cheating—which is ridiculous since he doesn't have romantic relationships. And this person suggests Cal should be punished for his behavior."

"Fuck. Does he have any idea who's sending these? A former lover?"

"You know Cal. One and done. He doesn't even sleep with the same person twice. How would he tick someone off that much? And how did this person get his number?" Ryker shook his head. "I've got a bad feeling about this situation."

Mac paced back and forth. "I don't like the sound of it either. Is there anything we can do?"

Ryker let out a sigh. "I gave him the rundown already. For now, it's sort of like spam. Weird and annoying, but not necessarily illegal. He needs to keep tabs and be smart about where he goes and who he's with. But I think we should take turns checking in with him every day, just to be safe."

"Agreed. Thanks for the heads-up. Cal may want to consider hiring a PI to see if anyone's been following him. Just a thought." Mac stopped pacing to stare out at the Manhattan skyline.

"Not a bad idea. You can tell him, but knowing Cal, he'll refuse," Ryker said. "On another topic, I noticed you and Wes having a rather involved conversation at dinner. You wanna bring me up to speed?" He held his breath, waiting for the answer.

Mac smiled and shook his head. "He just wanted to know more about you. I told him to ask you instead, but that means having an actual conversation with him, not giving him an ultimatum and walking away."

"I wasn't expecting to have a conversation with him tonight, Mac. You could have given me fair warning that he'd be here," Ryker countered, his body tense and rigid.

"If I had, you would have refused to come. Ry, come on. I know you. Please, please just talk to Wes. Get to know him a bit and see if the book series might be worth considering." Mac's rare but effective pleading look was Ryker's undoing. He could never say no to Mac's sad face, and tonight was proving to be no exception. *Fuck me!*

"Okay, okay. Don't beg. It's beneath you. Send

him up here and I'll force myself to talk to him." Ryker paused and gestured at the cigarette in his hand. "But if he makes a comment about my one smoke for the month, that's it." He chuckled darkly and watched as Mac gave a wave and headed back downstairs.

Ryker finished his cigarette and walked over to the lounger at the far corner of the patio. He sat down and leaned all the way back, closing his eyes to take in the sounds of the city streets below. The white noise of it lulled him into a relaxed state, until the familiar sounds and smells of the city were suddenly overpowered by citrus and salt, reminding Ryker of a day by the sea. He recognized that distinctive smell from earlier in the night.

"Wake up, Sleeping Beauty. Your Prince Charming has arrived."

****

Wes

While having coffee in the living room, Wes had noticed Ryker slip out. He wondered where Ryker was going, and his gut clenched when he thought he might be leaving the party. Despite some interesting conversations over dinner with various guests, Wes's attention kept veering back to Ryker and those telling cobalt eyes.

Ryker might be quiet in nature, but his beautiful eyes—wide and expressive—spoke volumes. Wes could tell the man had a lot to say. He just needed to know how to draw it out. For some reason he'd yet to understand, Wes wanted to get to know Ryker, book deal or not. He'd think about the why of that later.

So, here he was, silently slipping up to the rooftop patio thanks to Mac's directions.

Ryker was lying on one of the teak patio loungers, his long body stretched out, with one leg bent. With his eyes closed and a small smile in place, Ryker's face was the picture of serenity. The tiny stringed lights overhead winked and cast a soft glow on Ryker's profile, highlighting the dark stubble on his smooth skin and lips so lush they gave Wes the dirtiest of thoughts. The taut lines of Ryker's arms and legs strained under his sleek clothes, and Wes could so easily picture him naked in the very same pose. Waiting. Anticipating.

Fuck. Stop staring at the hot man. You've seen plenty of them, Wes reminded himself. He took a few deep breaths and, once he got himself back under a semblance of control, sauntered up to the lounger. He could smell the spicy scent that was uniquely Ryker, mixed in with something else. Tobacco?

"Wake up, Sleeping Beauty. Your Prince Charming has arrived," Wes said.

"I'm awake, Wes, and a beauty, I am not." Ryker opened his eyes and pushed himself up to a sitting position in one smooth movement, then ran his hands over his hair, which fell in messy waves around his shoulders. "And you're no Prince Charming, but you certainly have the ego of one."

"I think you're too modest, Ryker. Although if you continue with the smoking…" Wes chuckled and Ryker's fuck-off expression emerged again. Maybe Wes needed to dial back the smart-ass comments just a bit and focus more on honesty. Ryker would respect that, right?

Wes sat down on the lounger across from Ryker, staring straight into his eyes. "I'm no prince, but I do admit to my ego. I come by it honestly. My work speaks for itself."

Ryker's eyes were still cool but growing warmer, so Wes continued. "So, I've admitted I'm conceited, and you've admitted you like that about me—"

Ryker's burst of incredulous laughter surprised Wes, who couldn't help but stare at the way Ryker's smile transformed his face. This Sleeping Beauty was even more stunning than at first glance. Wes's blood thrummed, his heart beating a wild rhythm, and his dick grew hard despite the confines of his slim dress pants.

"I actually haven't admitted that, but I guess you're starting to grow on me," Ryker said. "Like mold."

"Eh, I've been called worse." Wes shrugged and grinned in response. "Can we have an actual conversation? Let's head back inside to talk. It's a bit chilly at this time of night."

Ryker got up and stopped right in front of Wes, touching his suit lapel—or rather, straightening it out. The heat of Ryker's fingers burned through the expensive material like a brand, and Wes wondered if Ryker felt the same electricity. Wes stared at those haunting blue eyes, and his heartbeat pulsed double time. Wes leaned closer to those sinful lips. *Maybe just one taste.*

And then Wes found himself alone again when Ryker abruptly stepped back and headed for the stairs, turning at the last minute.

"Okay, Wes," Ryker said. "But I warn you, I'm still not sold on this book series. You're going to have to do your best to convince me. I'm a stubborn pain in the ass who likes his routine."

The mention of the book deal broke Wes out of his sexual haze. Yes, the books. After all, that was the reason he was here. He'd better lock this sexual tension away and focus on his other desires. Like writing.

He smiled at Ryker with his cockiest grin and motioned to the doors. "Lead the way."

****

Ryker

Holy hell, I was thirty seconds away from kissing Wes. What is wrong with me?

It seemed Ryker's hormones had a mind of their own around Wes, despite knowing that the man was trouble. A well-intentioned touch to straighten Wes's lapel had backfired when Ryker felt the heat of Wes's solid chest. Standing that close, Ryker had wanted to kiss the freckles that dotted Wes's sharp nose and cheekbones before moving his way down to the full lips that beckoned with their softness. His blood had rushed south so fast that Ryker had to turn suddenly toward the patio doors so Wes wouldn't see the bulge in his now extra-tight jeans. *Ouch. Serves you right, almost kissing him. What the fuck were you thinking?*

Ryker hadn't had a hookup in months, so that had to be it. *It's just a reaction to prolonged frustration.* It wasn't like he was suddenly tempted by this blond-haired devil; he was just horny.

Ryker walked down to Mac's living room, which was now empty, and grabbed a spot on the sectional, Wes following suit.

"So, why don't you work well with others? And why the dirty look when you saw me for the first time tonight?" Wes asked.

"I did some research on you, and while I respect your early work, I'm not keen on the fact that you publicize your life. That's the complete opposite of me. And I was angry that I was ambushed tonight. I didn't know you'd be here."

"I can't speak as to why Mac didn't tell you. But don't dismiss this project based on faulty assumptions about who I am personally instead of the quality of my work."

"I'm not making assumptions. I look at the facts." Ryker's face flushed. "Most of your social media is about parties rather than your writing. That's not me. I care about my work and it comes first. It is my reason for being. I just don't think that you and I would be a good match given our differences in priorities."

"My priority is writing the best book I can, whether fiction or non-fiction. But being in the media is also part of my job. That's what generates sales. Come on, Ryker, you know this."

Ryker flinched. "I'm sure there are other writers who would love the opportunity to work with you. I suggest you talk to Mac about finding a more suitable partner for this collaboration."

Wes started to talk, but Ryker raised a hand to stop him. "I value privacy as well as honesty," he went on. "And I had a really bad experience with a colleague back when I was a journalist. I won't bore you with the details, but I really don't think we'd be a good fit working together."

Wes crossed his arms over his expansive chest and cocked his head, studying Ryker for several moments, his hazel eyes suddenly dark and serious. "I'm going to share something personal with you, something I haven't told anyone but Grey." Wes paused and ran a hand over his blond hair, down his neck, and then over his square jaw, looking uncomfortable for the first time that evening.

"I'm hitting a wall when it comes to my writing. The self-help books have done well for me, and I used to love everything that came with it. But lately, I'm not inspired to write much of anything. And that has to change. Writing has been my salvation since I was a kid. It was my escape, and then my ticket to a better life. But lately... I can't describe to you the stress I feel when I sit down and I have nothing to say. Nothing worth publishing, anyway. When Mac called me about this idea, I had a gut reaction that this was the answer I was searching for. So my motives are selfish, to be sure. But I promise you, I'm the hardest-working writer you'll ever collaborate with, and I mean what I say. I'm not shy. And I don't lie. Feel free to ask around."

"I'm sorry you're going through that, Wes. But I don't know that this changes my opinion about working together. I rely on my routine." Ryker paused. "I have a set way of doing things when I sit down to write a novel. I need it that way."

"I understand that, but you work with an editor. You have beta readers. You work with several people to create your final published work. It's not just you in a vacuum."

Ryker pondered Wes's comment for a moment. "True. But I've done most of the work and then it's adjustments. I don't know if I'm capable or willing to share my creative process with another writer."

"How do you know unless you try?"

There was a quiet pause in the room when Wes finished talking, and neither of them looked away.

Ryker wondered if he should take this chance. Would it be worth the anxiety he was feeling? Mac kept encouraging him to get out of his comfort zone and take creative risks. Maybe this was the time for that to happen. Or maybe he was about to make another big mistake.

"I'm still not convinced," Ryker said. "I think we ought to get to know each other first. We can meet up while you're in town and work on a few creative pieces to see if we're a good match. A book series is a serious commitment, and we both have to buy in one hundred percent to make it successful. And I don't do anything halfway."

Wes nodded. "Sounds fair."

"Good, stop by my place Monday morning for our first meeting. Give me your number and I'll text you the details."

"Done," Wes replied confidently.

"Oh, and one other thing."

"Name it."

"I want you to meet my mother," Ryker said with a smirk on his face.

Wes's shocked expression was priceless.

Chapter Seven
Wes

His mother? Wes was not expecting that. It seemed odd to meet the parents in this scenario, but if that was what it took, he would do it. Wes agreed and they finalized the details for a Monday meetup. Wes then texted Luca to re-book his flight and get his hotel stay extended for another few days.

As he finished entering the meeting details into his phone, Wes looked up to watch Ryker hug Mac and Cal goodbye. Ryker turned his head at the last moment before leaving, and the impact when those expansive blue eyes met his couldn't be denied. Fuck, if he wasn't careful, he could lose himself in those dark depths.

The sexual chemistry with Ryker was clear, but it made Wes somewhat uneasy, which wasn't like him. Normally, he went after men he desired, and then he moved on after his need was satisfied. But something about the way he reacted to Ryker at first sight was different. It was stronger, sharper than anything he'd felt before, and that scared the shit out of him. Maybe working together was a bad idea. Maybe having a few days to think it over was really for the best—for both of them. Or maybe he should take Ryker's advice and find someone else to work with.

It wasn't like Wes to second guess himself. The meeting was set, so he'd follow through. Shaking himself out of his weird mood, Wes walked over to Cal, Mac, and Grey. It was half past midnight, and all the other guests had left. And now that the object of Wes's distraction had gone, he was left feeling restless again.

"Okay, people. Time to have some real fun! Let's hit a club." Wes clapped his hands and rubbed them together, and all three sets of eyes landed on him. "We're young and single and ready to mingle!"

"Fuck yeah," Cal murmured, while Mac and Grey rolled their eyes.

"Please tell me you don't talk crap like that when you're trying to pick up men." Grey laughed and nudged Wes as they all made their way out Mac's door.

Wes winked. "Nah, I don't need to say anything."

They hopped in Cal's limo and, thanks to Mac's connections, scored a VIP lounge at The Royale, a popular Manhattan nightclub. With a view to the dance floor below, Wes felt his mood lighten as he watched all the pretty people at play. Many handsome men were writhing and grinding together on the dance floor, the beat of the house music and the dark purple lighting creating just the right seductive atmosphere. For a moment, he wished Ryker had joined them. But that might've complicated things, and Wes didn't want to think about Ryker when he had other, less troublesome options to choose from.

Determined to have some sexy fun, Wes scanned the crowd for his man of the night. When no one in particular caught his eye, he turned around to find Grey sitting alone with his head down, reading his phone. Cal and Mac were already heading down to the dance floor. Wes went over to sit beside Grey, nudging his arm.

"We don't have to stay long, Grey. I just wanted to dance a bit and see if someone catches my eye. You okay here, or do you want to leave?" As much as Wes wanted some fast, sweaty sex, his friend came first.

"I'm okay, but it's been a long time since I set foot in a club. Even though it would probably do me good to let loose and forget real life for a while, I don't know if I have the courage to go down there." Grey sighed and rubbed a hand down his face, then unbuttoned the top two buttons of his white shirt.

"Come on." Wes smiled and urged his friend to his feet. "Let's dance."

A short while later, all four men were at the center of the dance floor. Grey and Cal were dancing and laughing together. Mac had his arms wrapped around a slim guy with pink hair, and Wes was rubbing up against a handsome twenty-something man with long brown hair and lots of tattoos.

Wes couldn't help but compare the sexual pull he felt toward Ryker with the man he was now dancing with—John? Joshua? Jared? Shit, what was his name? Jay. He'd stick with that.

Jay was young and hot, but Wes wasn't totally into him, and he had no idea why. They'd groped each other and grinded together in a bid to get as close as possible, and it felt good, but nothing like the heat Wes felt from one single touch from Ryker. *Forget about him.*

"Let's get out of here and have some real fun together," Jay whispered in Wes's ear.

Wes glanced around and noticed that Cal was surrounded by a well-dressed blond man and a red-haired woman, and that Grey had slid away and was now headed up the stairs. Cal turned to follow Grey's movement until the blond man wrapped his big arms around Cal's waist and whispered something in his ear that made Cal laugh, and the new threesome continued dancing.

"Let me just check with my friend. I'll meet you out front in ten minutes," Wes said to Jay, and then weaved his way over to Mac. "I'm heading out. Thanks for tonight, Mac. I'll let you know how Monday goes with Ryker." And with a handshake and a nod, he was off.

He headed back to the VIP lounge and found Grey sitting in a large leather chair in the corner of the room, throwing back shots. Grey's right hand shook slightly, but when he looked up at Wes, his face was calm and smiling.

"Let's head back to the hotel. I've got my playdate for the night waiting out front, and you're probably done here, eh?" Grey nodded, and they headed for the exit.

Wes spotted Jay waiting just outside the main doors, leaning against the wall and smoking a cigarette as he chatted with another man. Under the streetlight, everything around Wes was sharper, clearer. And while Wes was still horny, it seemed that whatever minimal heat he'd felt when he looked at Jay on the dance floor was already starting to dissipate. Wes just wanted to get back to the hotel and go to sleep.

What the hell is wrong with me tonight? Ugh. I must be overtired.

"Hold on, Grey. I'll be right back."

He sauntered over to Jay and nodded. "Hey. I'm wiped out, so let's just call it a night right here. I had fun. Take care." He reached out to shake Jay's hand, but Jay just stared.

"No worries. I had fun, too," he replied with a shrug, then returned to his conversation with the other man. With that, Wes and Grey hopped in their rideshare.

"So, no action tonight?" Grey asked. "I thought you had a sure thing with that guy?"

"Yeah. I was enjoying myself for a bit, but then once I headed outside, I don't know. I guess I'm overtired," Wes murmured, staring out the window. He didn't know what else to say. For the second time tonight, he was at a loss for words, and it made him really fucking uncomfortable.

Grey was kind enough not to ask any more questions, and the rest of the ride passed in silence until they got to the hotel.

"I'm going to have a nightcap. You want to join me?" Grey asked, pointing to the lobby bar, but Wes shook his head. "Okay. We've got brunch and an interview tomorrow, so stop by my room around eleven?"

"Sounds good, Grey. Night." And with a wave, Wes found himself staring at his tired reflection in the hotel elevator. A few minutes later, he was back in his suite on the twenty-third floor.

Shrugging off his suit jacket, Wes headed into the bathroom and took off the rest of his clothes. A hot shower was just what he needed to wash off the sweat from the club. Once he was inside the large glass enclosure, the steam began to rise and Wes's body relaxed.

His mind kept going back to the rooftop patio earlier this evening. Ryker had stepped into his personal space and touched him unexpectedly, and combined with the effect of those big blue eyes, it had been all Wes could do to stop himself from reaching out and kissing him. *Fuck.*

Wes soaped up his heavy balls and stroked himself, tugging his now rock-hard cock with increasing urgency. A vision of Ryker kneeling before him was so clear, his dark hair wet and slick, his lush, sexy lips surrounding the swollen length of Wes's thick cock. He could hear Ryker's moan of satisfaction while he licked and sucked, could feel the coarse stubble of Ryker's cheek rubbing against his thigh, the roughness adding to the sensations pulsing through him.

Those eyes would look up at him, dark and sultry with lust. Ryker would take him deeper down his throat, moaning and sucking so hard, so good. Then he would tug on Wes's balls and slowly slide a finger up, up into his ass. Wes could no longer hold his orgasm at bay.

"Ah, fuck, Ryker! Yes!" Wes yelled as jet after jet of his hot cum covered the black tiles in the shower.

Bracing a shaky hand on the wall, Wes took several deep breaths to get his heart rate and breathing under control. *Jesus, I haven't come that hard or that quick in a while.* Once he had washed away the remains of his orgasm, Wes dried off and padded out to the bedroom, slipping under the covers of his king-sized bed.

He checked his phone. There was one text at two fifteen AM. Speaking of the dark angel.

Ryker: **Don't forget to bring bagels on Monday. Sadie's, 463 W Broadway in SoHo. And I hope you aren't allergic to dogs or cats. I have both.**

It was sent ten minutes ago. Should he reply?

Wes smiled to himself and started typing: **So demanding. Are you going to be this bossy for our whole collaboration? If bagels keep you happy, I'll get a daily delivery. And I have a dog myself so pets are NP.**

Ryker: **I haven't agreed to the book deal yet. And you really have a dog? How come he/she isn't in any of your social media posts? Afraid they'll steal your spotlight?**

Wes: **Yup, Peanut's way cuter than me. I can't let him have all the attention. And you said "yet." You'll be so happy working with me you'll wonder why you said no in the first place.**

Ryker: **☐ Your ego is so big, I'm surprised Peanut has room to live with you.**

Wes: **He loves me. I'm irresistible☐**

Shit, stop flirting, he reprimanded himself.

Ryker: **See you Monday. Lots to discuss.**

Wes: **I'll be there, Ry. Can I call you Ry?**

Ryker: **Sure, easier for you to remember in that**

BIG head of yours ☐ **Also, when you wake up tomorrow (or I guess today, given the time), write a short story, 500 words, and e-mail it to me. Mac has my details. Night.**

Wes: **Homework? r u joking?**

Ryker: **Nope. Don't disobey the teacher. Sweet dreams, Wes.**

Wes couldn't help the huge grin on his face. He could think of so many naughty replies to Ryker's last text, but he left it at that. Ryker was smart and sarcastic, and sparring with him was stimulating in more ways than one. Controlling his flirting tendencies around him might prove difficult, though, since Wes enjoyed their teasing banter more than he should. He hoped the same stimulation would apply to their potential collaboration. If they played off their differences, it could result in something truly special.

Wes finally placed his phone on the nightstand and turned off the bedside lamp. Despite the blackout curtains, some of the light from the city filtered in through the edges, casting a soft glow over the cream-colored bedspread. Wes slowly drifted off, hoping his writing muse would once again start to whisper to him in his dreams.

He had a feeling his muse was now a hot, grumpy New Yorker with long, black hair and blue eyes. He could work with that.

Chapter Eight
Ryker

Ryker couldn't sleep. Again.

This time it wasn't anxiety keeping him awake. He was just fucking horny. He'd come so close to picking up the phone and calling Wes instead of texting him. God knows why. *Just to hear that deep, sexy voice say my name, that's why.* This whole thing with Wes was bad—this book collaboration, their crazy chemistry, the texting and flirting. Bad, bad, bad.

But it sure as hell didn't stop Ryker from fantasizing. He stretched out on his bed and reached down to his black briefs, shoving them down his thighs and taking himself in hand. He reached for the lube in the nightstand drawer with his left hand while his right continued to jack his now very erect cock.

Shit, that lube is cold. Pre-cum slipped out his slit, and Ryker used it and the added lube to create a warm, slick slide.

A minute later, his cock—along with the rest of his body—was so hot, Ryker thought the bedsheets would combust. He imagined Wes here with him, lying on his California king bed, all six feet of his big, muscular body stretched out naked for Ryker to explore.

He'd start with Wes's pecs, since he was sure Wes had a phenomenal chest. At least, it felt that way under his suit tonight. Ryker would then slowly run his fingers through Wes's blond chest hair—please, God, let him have chest hair—and over solid muscle to his nipples, tugging first, then bending over to lick and gently bite as Wes swore and panted his demands.

"That's it, Ry. Don't stop."

Finding a sensitive spot, Ryker did as he was told

and tugged harder on Wes's flat brown nipples, the grunts and groans of Wes's satisfaction spurring him on. He then slowly licked his way down to Wes's navel, gently biting and kissing the skin that was smooth and sprinkled with more blond hair. Wes's skin was salty and musky, the taste so primal that it made Ryker's cock even harder. Ryker then took both their dicks in hand and jacked them off together, their combined pre-cum creating a messy, sticky friction that was so damn good.

"Ry," Wes moaned and gripped his ass, sliding his fingers over his sensitive hole. "I'm going to pound your perfect ass. Fuck you hard until you scream my name."

Holy shit, just the thought of Wes sliding into his tight hole was enough to send his fantasy right over the edge.

"Wes!" Ryker groaned loudly and came so hard he thought he might black out. He'd probably woken the neighbors on this floor and the one below with his shouting. *Jesus, that was powerful.* He couldn't remember the last time he'd experienced such an amazing orgasm. *Too fucking long.*

When Ryker finally and reluctantly opened his eyes, he found himself in the real world again, alone, the sheets cold and messy with his cum.

Thirty minutes later, with clean sheets and an exhausted body, he finally got back into bed and turned on his sleep app. Now that the room was free of sex noises, his fur babies slowly wandered in and hopped onto the bed beside him. Thoughts of the evening swirled in the back of his mind, but Ryker refused to let his sleep be interrupted by Wes again. Ryker had worked Wes out of his system with his nighttime fantasy, and now things would be back to normal. No more flirting or eye fucking. He could focus on testing out this collaboration in a strictly professional way. Right?

Wes's deep chuckle reverberated in his memory. *Fuck.*

****

Wes

Sunday morning came too quickly. And too loudly, thanks to Wes's hotel neighbors down the hall, who seemed to be having a really fucking good time until six in the morning. Emphasis on the fucking.

Much as he hated the disturbance to his sleep, Wes was both aroused and envious. The noise-fest did not help his morning hard-on. Neither did thinking of his dark-eyed writing partner and imagining what he would sound like in the same scenario. *Stop thinking about Ryker!*

Before he gave in to his baser instincts again, he remembered Ryker's request and grabbed his laptop. First, he contacted Mac and got Ryker's address. Then he started his "homework." Surprisingly, the words flowed out of him this morning. Before he knew it, over an hour had passed and he'd written just over seven hundred words, then jotted down some ideas about potential plots for their series. New York City's energetic vibes were rubbing off on him already.

Speaking of rubbing off, his mind wandered back to the shower last night. *No, focus.*

Needing a distraction that would energize him for his live interview at eleven, Wes threw on his running gear and headed for the elevator. The hotel had a fully equipped gym that was usually empty at eight on a Sunday morning, so a run on the treadmill was in order.

Wes glanced down to the end of the long hallway and noticed a man leaving Grey's room.

Probably room service. Wait—no hotel uniform.

Probably a business meeting. Wes walked a few steps closer to get a better look at the man.

Blond, slim, wearing a white shirt that looked two sizes too big. Wes couldn't make out the man's face from this distance, but his profile looked familiar.

Before Wes could move or say anything, the man rushed off to the elevator and was gone. *None of my business anyway.*

Two hours later, Wes was back in his room, freshly showered and enjoying his first coffee when his phone rang: Grey.

"Hey, bud, hold on." He gulped down the rest of his brew. "I'm just having coffee, but I still need to get dressed. I'll drop by your suite in ten minutes."

Grey cleared his throat. "Sure. How did you sleep?"

"Not much, but that's hotels for you. At least some people on this floor had sexy fun last night. Or I should say early this morning. Fuck, they were loud. Did they wake you up, too?" Wes asked, and Grey coughed on the other end of the line. "You all right, Grey? I hope you haven't caught a bug."

More throat clearing from Grey. "No, just allergies. You know the way it is this time of year. Okay, well, see you soon," he said, then hung up.

Once Wes was ready, he knocked on Grey's door and they headed off for a quick brunch and then the interview.

His spot on *Weekend New York* was better than Wes had expected. The anchor, Haley Sanders, was professional and charming, drawing her audience in with funny questions and quips. Wes couldn't remember the last time he'd felt so relaxed in an interview. Not that it was a hardship—he loved people, and talking about his work helping other writers find their voice was rewarding. At least, it had been for the past several years. Funny he should be in a position now to need his own advice since his creative mojo was on hiatus.

Haley led into the final questions. "So tell me, Wes, now that *My 90-Day Novel* is a bestseller, what's next on your list? Are you going to go back to writing fiction? I, for one, am a huge fan of your Darren Fields mysteries, and I'm dying to know—pun intended—" She paused as the audience laughed. "—if we're going to see any further books. I won't give too much away in case some of our audience hasn't read it yet, but in the last book, Darren faced an unresolved personal conflict."

Wes smiled. "As you know, Haley, New York City is my first stop on a tour across the US for *My 90-Day Novel,* and then it's back home to Toronto for a much-needed rest. We'll see what happens in a few months. I've been mulling new ideas, so I'll have to get back to you. But I appreciate all the love for my mysteries. They were a joy to write, and I hope a joy to read."

"Indeed. Rumor has it that you're working with another well-known author on a new series. Any truth to that? And if so, what kind of series?" Haley asked.

How the hell had she gotten ahold of that information? Good thing Wes was a pro at improvising.

"Rumors are just that. You don't believe everything you read about me in the tabloids, do you, Haley?" Wes laughed and put on his best-selling grin.

"Well, I've read some pretty spicy things about you, so I hope so. Speaking of which, you were photographed entering a nightclub this weekend with New York City's most eligible gay socialite, Mac Duran. Are you two an item?" she asked, leaning forward in anticipation of his response.

Ah, now Wes realized how she'd made the

supposition about his new project. Wes smiled at the audience. "Like I said, don't believe everything you read. Well, my books are the exception." He paused to let the low ripple of audience laughter flow over him. "I know lots of people, and I like to socialize. And I certainly don't hide my sexuality, but some things still should remain private."

Wes hoped that would put an end to a line of questioning that was starting to make him uncomfortable.

Haley turned back to Wes. "Well, it's been great having you here, Wes, and we look forward to your next book. Come back and visit us again when you're in town." Haley quickly turned and smiled at the audience. "I hope all of you have enjoyed today's guests. Have a great Sunday and a wonderful week ahead! Take care, New York." And with that, the cameras turned off and the lights dimmed.

Haley touched Wes's arm. "Great job, Wes. I hope you didn't mind the personal question. You know how it is in this business. Everyone's vying for the latest juicy piece of news."

"Of course, Haley. No harm, no foul. Thank you again." He shook Haley's hand and set out for the exit.

No, he didn't mind. He was used to it. He just hoped his potential new writing partner wouldn't mind either.

Chapter Nine
Ryker

Ryker was mesmerized by Wes's TV interview.

Much as he loathed this type of thing, he had to admit that Wes was very good at the public relations stuff. He had charisma to spare.

When the topic of the book collaboration came up, he could see the momentary flicker of unease on Wes's face. *How the hell did she get that information?* Wes's jaw clenched before he resumed that practiced smile and turned the tables on the interviewer. And then there was that comment about Mac.

If that had been me, I would've told her to fuck off and walked right off the set.

Was it possible there was something between Wes and Mac? Wes hadn't fully acknowledged the rumor, but he hadn't squelched it either. That was probably how you had to play the media game to keep them guessing and hold their attention. But just the thought of Wes and Mac being intimate together made Ryker's stomach revolt.

Pushing that thought, and the interview, aside, Ryker went back to work. Several hours later, and after all his revisions were complete, Ryker was standing in the kitchen, prepping a chicken and veggie stir fry, when his phone beeped.

Mac: **You got a few minutes to chat?**

Ryker: **Yup.**

His phone rang almost immediately.

"Hey, what's up?" Ryker answered on speakerphone while chopping zucchini and carrots, occasionally throwing Spock a piece of food to avoid his sad but persistent stare-down.

"I've reached out to Wes's assistant to set up a

conference call for tomorrow at seven PM. I thought we'd formalize a few things."

"Aren't you jumping the gun, Mac? Or maybe you just want to talk to Wes again, since apparently you two are an item now?" Ryker commented, only half joking.

Mac snorted. "Yeah, no. Wait, you watched the interview today? Taking a new interest in daytime TV, Ry?"

"Research. I need to learn all I can about Wes so I can make an informed decision. You know me. Logical and practical. And Mac, Wes and I need to get to know each other and do some work together before we can say yes. This is a big deal for me. For both of us."

"Well, that's good. I'm so glad your previous 'no way' is now 'an informed decision.' I'm going to chill the champagne just in case. I'll text you the details for tomorrow. Call your agent! Ciao."

Mac's call reminded him of something else he had to do. Ryker picked up his phone again.

"Hey, how are you? Good. Listen, I have a favor to ask. Can you be here tomorrow morning at nine thirty? I'd like to introduce you to someone." He paused. "No, not in that way. Have you ever known me to do that? This is business. I'll call you later with more details. Okay, thanks."

Ryker's gut tightened at the thought of seeing Wes again. Was it apprehension or pleasure? Admittedly, a little bit of both.

****

Wes

Rush hour on a Monday morning in New York City was frenetic and entertaining. Wall-to-wall traffic and masses of people pushing to get ahead—and that was just the line at the bagel shop.

This was Wes's first time at Sadie's in SoHo, and what a revelation. The sweet aroma of freshly baked bread, toasted sesame seeds, and other spices wafted through the vintage bakery. Wes waited twenty minutes for his delicious-smelling order: six sesame seed and six poppy seed bagels, along with a container of cream cheese and homemade lox.

What should have been a five-minute ride from the bagel shop to Ryker's took almost half an hour due to gridlock. *Next time I'll walk. If there is a next time.* Luckily, he still arrived ten minutes early. Being late was one of Wes's few pet peeves.

Stepping out of the car, Wes glanced up at his destination, a stylish old building on Park Avenue with ornate stonework and large windows that looked out over one of the world's most iconic places: Central Park. Wes had pictured Ryker in some industrial loft in Brooklyn, but he couldn't deny the appeal of this location.

Wes gave his name to the concierge, added his details to the security system, and was then escorted to the elevator. Exiting on the twenty-eighth floor, he walked down a narrow hallway lit with bronze wall sconces until he reached Ryker's door.

Wes knocked twice, and a barrage of barking and footsteps could be heard behind the door. A flutter in his stomach took flight. A combination of nerves, hunger, and some other form of anticipation filled him, and he took a deep breath. He smoothed down his olive-green Henley. He'd opted for a casual look today with black jeans and boots.

When the door opened, Wes was greeted by a smiling woman in her fifties. She was petite and very beautiful. With long, dark hair, wide brown eyes, and a smile that was now familiar to him, he eagerly put out his hand.

"*Hola*, Mr. Stewart, come in. I'm Tina Desoumas, Ryker's mother. It's a pleasure to meet you. I'm a big fan of your books." She gripped Wes's hand firmly, her hand lightly calloused, warm, and very strong. She couldn't have been more than five-foot-five and was curvaceous in stylish black yoga pants and a long, white button-down shirt. Her feet were bare, displaying dark blue nail polish. Beside her stood a small dog with big pointy ears, his sleek black-and-brown pelt shimmying as he wagged his tiny tail.

"This is Spock, and he's also very excited to meet you, as you can tell." She laughed as the miniature pinscher stood on his back legs to reach up and lick Wes's hand.

"Chances are he's more excited about the food smells than seeing me," Wes replied as he held up the large brown bag. "And thank you, Tina, the pleasure is all mine. I hope I'm not too early. I've brought breakfast," he said as he followed her down the hallway into Ryker's modern apartment, reaching the kitchen.

Tina's eyes widened. "Ryker made you bring food?" She turned toward the kitchen and yelled, "Ryker! *Qué hiciste? Es un invitado en tu casa!*"

Wes wasn't fluent in Spanish, but he knew a pissed-off mother when he heard one. Ryker appeared at the end of the kitchen counter, arranging cups and other items for coffee. A lovely flush of color bloomed over his cheekbones, his dark hair sliding over his shoulders in silky waves that Wes was suddenly very eager to bury his hands in. Wes's gaze slid down Ryker's form, taking in the square, black-rimmed glasses that perfectly framed his indigo eyes, his lean body in a black t-shirt and tight faded jeans, and all the way down to his bare feet.

When Wes's eyes roamed up again to meet

Ryker's, the impact was undeniable. Wes acknowledged that he'd never been so physically aroused by anyone in his life. He had an overwhelming urge to grab Ryker's stunning face in both hands and kiss him, right the fuck now, not caring that his mother was two feet away. Wes didn't believe in love at first sight—but lust was pretty close.

"Mama, it was a joke. I didn't think he would take it seriously," Ryker countered, looking bashful. "But thank you, Wes."

"No problem. You did text me their address, so I assumed you were serious," Wes replied with a grin. "And I didn't mind at all. I love discovering new shops and restaurants in New York City, and this place will earn a repeat visit," he said, taking a seat on one of the black leather bar stools at the far end of the counter.

"My son, I will admit, he is smart. So clever. But sometimes smart ass is more like it." Tina grabbed a navy-blue dish towel hanging from the oven door and swatted Ryker on said ass. *Lucky towel*, Wes thought.

Tina smiled and turned back to him. "Wes, we're having *café con leche*, a sweet latte, but Ryker has one of those machines that can make fifty types of coffee and tea, so you can have whatever pleases you." She waved at the gleaming coffee machine.

"I'll have *café con leche* as well, please and thanks," Wes answered.

He watched Ryker as he bit his full lower lip in concentration, adjusting the machine with strong, practiced hands. Ryker's long, fluid body moved quietly in the kitchen space. Wes would be happy to stare at this sexy man all day, but Tina interrupted his lustful daydream.

"So well mannered. It is very rare these days. You were brought up right," she said to Wes as she placed the bagels and cream cheese on a platter. "Please help yourself, Wes."

"Thank you. My grandmother did her best," Wes said as he took a sesame bagel and spread it generously with cream cheese. Ryker finished making the coffees and placed them on the counter, then took a seat on the stool beside Wes, his now familiar spicy scent wafting over. Wes sipped on his drink and murmured his appreciation. "Mmm, creamy and sweet. Best coffee I've ever had."

He looked at Ryker as the words left his mouth, and all he could think of was how Ryker would taste. Wes was glad he was sitting behind the counter so no one could see the prominent bulge in his jeans. He shifted in his seat to ease his discomfort and caught Ryker's smirk. So, the hot word nerd thought his predicament was funny, eh?

Wes raised his left eyebrow, then slowly licked cream cheese off his fingers one at a time, watching as Ryker's eyes locked on his mouth, his face flushing, his body slowly shifting on his seat, mirroring Wes. *Payback's a bitch*, Wes thought as he smirked back at him and winked.

Tina's eyes narrowed as she looked at Ryker, then Wes. She took a seat opposite them, and then a long sip of her *café*. "So, Wes, I understand that, just like my Ryker, you date men. Is your interest in him sexual, or is this purely business?"

Wes choked on his bagel, and Ryker spit out a mouthful of coffee, spewing droplets all over the glossy countertop. Tina laughed and shook her head at both of them.

Chapter Ten
Ryker

Asking his mother to come here had come back to bite Ryker on the ass.

He'd wanted to get her read on Wes. She was a hardworking, successful businesswoman, and Ryker trusted her instincts about people. She had, after all, learned the hard way since his father had up and left when Ryker was six months old.

He'd also wanted to make Wes a little bit uncomfortable, but that plan had backfired.

Despite his mom's presence this morning and his reaction to her frank question, Wes regained his composure quickly and was already back to his annoyingly charming self.

Wes chuckled. "You don't pull any punches, do you, Tina?"

"Forgive me for my timing, but I am very direct. I run a marketing agency, so as a businesswoman, I am used to getting right to the point to avoid wasting time. Time is precious, right?" she said with a smile.

"Yes, I'm that way, too." Wes paused, quickly glancing at Ryker before turning his attention back to Tina. "I won't deny that your son is extremely attractive, but I'm here to convince him to work with me. Ryker feels we won't mesh well because of our differences in personality. But I want to explore the potential for a creative partnership. I think combining our writing styles will bring forth an exciting venture. I'm also having some trouble with writer's block, and I'm hoping Ryker can help me. I respect his work immensely and feel that I could learn a lot from him."

Wes's words of praise made Ryker's heart beat

faster. He respected Wes's openness, but he was also surprised that Wes had revealed his writing problems again. It wasn't an easy thing to admit. As a writer, experiencing a block was so frustrating and, depending on how bad it was or how long it went on, terrifying. He knew it was difficult for Wes to tell anyone, let alone Ryker and now his mother, who was practically a stranger at this point.

Wes had also admitted that he found Ryker attractive, but maybe that was just for show. Wes was a natural flirt, so it was hard to tell. Ryker sensed that Wes's reactions were genuine. Ryker felt a pull between them and a tension he couldn't deny—it was natural and powerful. He hoped he wasn't alone in that feeling. Even as Ryker's rational brain issued warnings to stay away, he couldn't help but be drawn to Wes's energy.

"Well, thank you for your honesty, Wes." Tina smiled and gestured between them. "I think you two boys need to talk it out. I have a spa appointment in half an hour, so I have to get going." She stood, put her plate and cup in the sink, then walked back over to the counter and placed a hand on Wes's shoulder. "Wes, it was nice to meet you. Hopefully, we'll meet again for a longer discussion. In the meantime, I wish you the best of luck with my stubborn son. You will need it." She grabbed a large leather tote bag from the living room sectional, then waved and headed down the hallway. "Ryker, come help me with the door, please."

Ryker followed his mom, as requested, and held the door open for her.

"Ryker, you be kind to that man. He probably has the world at his feet, but there is something inside him that is lost. You can see it in his eyes. You are a quiet, caring soul. Be patient with Wes." Ryker started to respond, but Tina held a hand up to silence him and continued: "I know you were hurt in the past, but life is for living, and I want to see you happy and fulfilled. You spend too much time alone, *mi cariño*. It's not healthy. Now, go talk to your writing partner." She kissed him on the cheek and was off.

"He's not my partner yet," Ryker mumbled. He stood at the door until his mom disappeared into the elevator, then made his way back to the kitchen.

Only to find Isaac, the cat who didn't like anyone, curled up on Wes's lap as if he belonged there. Was there not one single being this man could not charm? Wes's large hand rubbed soothingly over Isaac's white fur, and Ryker found it strange that he was suddenly envious of his cat. Ryker imagined those warm palms rubbing over his skin, sparking fiery trails of excitement with every touch.

"Be careful. Isaac is prone to biting and scratching anyone but me," Ryker warned.

"Nah, we're cool. You love me, don't you, baby?" Wes cooed. Isaac's purrs grew louder, and then Princess Leia, the tabby, trotted into the room to see what all the fuss was about. "And who do we have here?" Wes asked as she started to rub against his legs.

"This is Princess Leia, but she acts like a queen. Very demanding," Ryker said as he picked Leia up and scratched her head. Spock sat by Wes's feet, curled up and content.

It was rare for Ryker to have company over, and he stood quietly watching Wes interact with his fur babies. He expected to feel awkward, but it never happened. It felt right to have Wes here in his space. Like he belonged. He would think about why later.

"I hope my mom didn't offend you," Ryker said, breaking the silence.

"Nope, she's great. I love a person who gets right

to the heart of the matter. Just out of curiosity, 'cause I am a nosy writer, do you have any more family?" Wes asked as he continued to cradle Isaac.

"My sister, Rachel. She lives in Australia. It's just the three of us. My dad left when I was six months old and Rachel was five." Ryker pointed to a photo of Rachel, his mom, and himself as a seven-year-old, standing in front of the New York City public library branch on Fifth Avenue. "My dad was in the army and met my mom when he was stationed in San Juan. They met, quickly married, moved here, had us and then, one day, five years later, he left. Mom spoke very little English at the time and had no job. She'd been a nurse in San Juan but couldn't get hired here. We struggled for many years. Thankfully, we had a nice neighbor who helped us out. Mom learned English, eventually got a job as an office assistant, and then earned a full scholarship to go back to school. And the rest is history." He paused. "Sorry, I don't know why I told you all that."

"I don't mind. Talk all you want. Feel free to tell me it's none of my business, but what happened to your dad?" Wes asked cautiously, placing Isaac on the floor, then rubbing his hands on his thighs.

"We don't know. Mom hired an investigator years later when she could afford it, but they never found him. My dad, Walter Hoffman, was born and raised in Vermont, so we thought maybe he'd gone back there but no. The investigator looked into his parents, who were from Germany, but my grandparents were both deceased by the time my father got married, and we didn't know of any other relatives. When we were older, Rachel and I took our mother's maiden name. I didn't really want to think of my dad or see the reminder of him every time I signed my name. And unlike Rachel, I don't have any memories of him."

Wes appeared to be at a loss for words. Ryker gave him a small smile. "Everything worked out. We've had each other and support from our friends. We're all hardworking, fairly well-adjusted people."

"I know a bit about where you're coming from. I was raised by my grandmother after my parents died. Well, you've already read my bio. My parents were murdered at their lakefront cabin when I was just eight."

Ryker nodded. "I'm so sorry, Wes. I can't imagine how you coped with that loss at such a young age."

"A lot of therapy and a lot of love from my grandmother. I didn't make it easy on her, though. When I was a teenager, I became obsessed with finding out what happened to my parents and answering the question that haunted me—why them?"

"Seems like we both had to deal with difficult unknowns."

Wes nodded in agreement. "Eventually, I got an answer, but it didn't make the grieving process any easier. Unfortunately, they were at the wrong place at the wrong time. The man who murdered them was living nearby and had mental health issues. He'd been experiencing increased paranoia and hallucinations, and he was convinced my parents were encroaching on his land and were out to hurt him. When I look back on it now, it makes me sad rather than angry at the whole situation. If only he'd received the help he needed, my parents might be alive."

"How did you cope with that knowledge?"

"It took a long time for me to process it, and I'm still not sure I'm done. I guess that's why I was always drawn to mysteries. I was curious about what drives people to desperate acts. I even thought about becoming an investigator at one point, but writing won out." Wes sighed and ran a hand over his face. "And now my memories of my parents get fainter as time goes on. Thank God for my grandmother. She kept all their mementos and pictures so at least I have that. My grandmother was strict with me, but she loved me fiercely. She was quite a woman—lively, outgoing, witty. Even after all the losses she'd suffered, she was determined to live life to the fullest."

"Sounds like her grandson," Ryker mused. This time it was Wes's turn to blush. Their eyes met and a powerful awareness passed between them. Ryker forced himself to look away.

Ryker switched gears, breaking the moment. "Do you mind if we turn back to the project? I was doing some brainstorming last night on possible themes for the book series. I thought we could each write a chapter and see how our styles mesh."

Ryker walked over to his storyboard wall and Wes followed, bringing with him the unique smell of salt and citrus Ryker loved. It made Ryker want to push Wes up against the nearest wall and lick his throat, to see if he tasted just as good as he smelled. After their personal revelations, and in the close confines of the apartment, Ryker's body craved a similar intimacy with Wes. He imagined sucking and nibbling up the side of his neck, over that blond stubble, until he reached those sumptuous lips. Then he would plunge his tongue into Wes's mouth, and they would battle for dominance, neither of them coming up for air until…

"You've been busy."

Wes's comment interrupted Ryker's vivid fantasy. "Insomnia leaves me with hours to do nothing but think and write," Ryker said, shrugging.

"How long have you been dealing with that?" Wes asked.

"For the past ten years," Ryker stated. "It's a long story. I might share it with you another day."

Two hours, three more cups of coffee, and four arguments later, Wes and Ryker had come up with a list of three possible plot tropes for their fantasy series.

"I want the relationship between the protagonists to be sexy and erotic. It should be sweaty, messy, and dirty. Emphasis on the dirty." Wes waggled his eyebrows.

Ryker ran his hands through his hair in frustration. "That's the one thing I'm worried about. I've never written sex scenes or romantic dialogue before. I'm going to have to do some research."

"Research? Just think of any fantasy you've had recently and write it down. Boom, done."

Ryker's face flushed an alarming shade of red, and Wes grinned. Recalling his earlier fantasy starring the man before him, Ryker already had one particular scene in mind.

"Okay, so the sex scenes may not be an issue. But the love story? The fuck do I know about romantic love? What about you?" Ryker looked expectantly at Wes.

Wes pursed his lips for a moment and then let out a big sigh, his golden eyes darker as they met Ryker's head-on. "I thought I was in love once. But it turned out to be a big fat lie. On his part. I was a fool. So, yeah, I don't know much about love either. Let's just focus on the major plot points and character development for now. We'll deal with the rest later."

Ryker nodded in agreement. "Do you have any plans this afternoon?" he asked.

"Nope. Why, are you asking me out on a date?" Wes said with a smirk.

Ryker rolled his eyes. "No, Prince Charming. Our call with Mac is at seven, so we have a few hours to kill and I've got an errand to run. Why don't you come with me? Then we can bring back dinner and take the call here."

"You're not going to ditch me in a bad part of town, are you? I'm a defenseless Canadian." Wes's eyes were back to their usual bright gleam.

Ryker made sure to keep a straight face. "You'll have to be brave and find out."

Chapter Eleven
Wes

Wes wasn't entirely surprised when they arrived at Heart2Home, an animal rescue shelter in midtown Manhattan. After all, Ryker housed three pets in a small New York apartment. His love of animals was evident.

A tall woman with a short blonde bob and blue eyes met them at the front desk. "You're in earlier than usual, Ry. And I see you've brought a guest?"

She moved around the desk to give Ryker a hug.

"This is a colleague of mine, Wes Stewart. He's going to be helping me out this afternoon. Wes, this is Charlotte Landing. She's the executive director of Heart2Home."

"Oh, my God! Of course I recognize Mr. Stewart! Welcome to our humble shelter. This is truly an honor. I'm such a big fan of your books." She gushed as she grasped Wes's hand tightly. "Wait, are you here for research? Are you writing a new mystery series? Oh! You could set one here and we could all be your suspects," she squealed.

"I'm just here as Ryker's guest, but you never know," Wes replied politely.

"You're here to volunteer with Ryker? That's so awesome," she smiled, turning to Ryker. "We've got three new dogs in this week. If you and Wes could sign in and take them for a walk, that would be super." She handed over a clipboard. "Oh, and Rudy is still nervous around new people. Maybe spend some one-on-one time with him again?"

"Sure thing," Ryker replied.

They signed in and wandered down a long hallway to a solid green door. As they approached it, Wes could hear all manner of barks, woofs, and meows coming from the other side. Ryker grabbed the clipboard that was hanging on the door and read aloud. "Okay, enclosures five, eight, and twelve are the new dogs. Let's take them for a walk, then come back and visit with Rudy."

"Who's Rudy?" Wes asked.

"He's a four-year-old golden retriever and German shepherd mix. Been here about a month. He was found locked in a cage, malnourished, and with signs of physical abuse. When he was first brought in, he barely looked at anyone. He tends to be nervous, especially around men, so talk softly, kneel down, and let him sniff your hand. And no sudden movements."

Ryker was totally comfortable and engaged in this environment. It was like Wes was seeing a different person compared to the man with the defensive posture he'd met at Mac's party. Though there was definitely something about Ryker's moodiness that made Wes want to tease him and draw out a smile. He had to admit he found both sides of Ryker's personality appealing. *Fuck me.*

A handsome young brunet man wearing red scrubs and a huge smile appeared at the door, interrupting Wes's musings. "Ry, so great to see you again. Here to visit the new brood?"

The man moved closer to Ryker, right up in his personal space, placing his hand on Ryker's arm and squeezing. *Take your hand off him,* Wes thought as his mood soured.

"Yup, it seems like quite the crowd today. Hopefully, you can find good homes for them soon. I take it they all passed the health check?" Ryker asked, slowly pulling away from the man and turning to Wes. "Sorry, Wes, this is Dr. Javier Rohas. He's the vet that visits the shelter once a week. Javier, Wes Stewart."

Javier stepped close to Wes and grasped his hand tightly. "So nice to meet a friend of Ry's. Do you live in town, or are you just visiting?" he asked, his blinding grin now reduced to a polite smile.

Wes responded carefully. "Visiting for now, but New York is my favorite city in the US. So who knows?" He smiled back.

Javier moved closer to Ryker again. "Ry, did Charlotte mention the benefit gala we're hosting next month for the shelter? We'd love for you to join us."

Ryker crossed his arms and shifted backward. "I don't know. I'd be happy to make a donation instead."

"But you're one of our foundational volunteers. We'd love for you to attend in person, maybe say a few words? It would mean the world to me. I mean, to us," Javier pleaded with his big eyes as he grabbed Ryker's arm again.

Wes rolled his eyes internally. Between the fluttering lashes routine and the way Javier kept touching Ryker's arm, could he be more obvious?

Ryker gracefully pulled his arm back and turned toward the door. Javier's eyes locked onto Ryker's jean-clad butt like a laser beam.

"I'll think about it," Ryker said.

"Great." Javier reached into his pocket and pulled out a card. "My personal number is at the bottom. Call or text me and we can make plans. For the benefit, I mean." Javier smirked at Wes, and Wes winked, getting a glare in return. Javier sauntered down the hallway. "Nice to meet you, Wes. Ryker, see you next week," he said in a cool, confident voice and headed out.

"Why doesn't that guy just say what he means?" Wes said.

"What are you talking about?" Ryker asked.

This time, Wes let his eye-roll out. "He wants to ask you out. The benefit is just an excuse."

Ryker's shook his head and rubbed his hands together. "You're crazy. He's just being nice."

"Nice doesn't touch your arm constantly. And nice doesn't stare at your ass. I saw actual drool coming out of Dr. Doolittle's mouth when you walked by him," Wes said, irritated at Javier for flirting and his own overreaction to it.

"Haha. It doesn't matter. I'm not interested. He's looking for a boyfriend, and I don't do repeats. And this place is special to me. I won't allow personal issues to interfere with it." Ryker grabbed leashes and plastic bags. "Come on, we have dogs to walk," he said, and that was the end of that conversation.

Wes forced himself to let his irrational jealousy go and clapped his hands together. "I'm ready, boss," he said as Ryker handed him the bags. "But why are you giving me ten bags?"

"You get to walk Furley, the mastiff, and Ned, the Great Dane. Big dogs make big..." Ryker trailed off, smiling.

Shit.

****

Ryker

Once they'd walked the dogs, they headed back to visit with Rudy. The beautiful golden-haired dog was sitting in the corner of his stall, curling his big body in a tight ball and watching Ryker and Wes with sad brown eyes. He started to whine and tremble, and Ryker immediately felt guilty about causing the animal distress. He opened the door slowly and sat on the floor with his hands resting on his legs.

"Hey, Rudy, how are you, buddy? Do you want to

come and say hi?" Ryker whispered. Rudy slowly uncurled his body and got up. The dog walked over hesitantly and quickly sniffed Ryker's hand but then ran back to his corner and whined.

"Some days are better than others, but it's taken him a long time to come near me. Would you like to try?" Ryker whispered to Wes.

Ryker slowly got up and moved silently out of the room. Wes took his place, but instead of sitting, he lay down on the floor on his stomach with his head propped on his hands. Rudy's tail slowly started to wag as he watched Wes lying silently on the floor. The dog then got up and walked over, sniffing Wes's head and hands and making his way down his body.

"That's a good boy, Rudy," Wes encouraged. "You're so brave and strong." Wes continued to whisper praise to the dog as Rudy's tail began to wag more vigorously. The dog eventually lay down beside Wes and poked his nose in his armpit, then moved on to Wes's ear, sniffling and licking, causing Wes to laugh softly. Ryker was tempted to take out his phone and snap a picture of the adorable sight in front of him, but he didn't want to scare Rudy with any sudden movements.

"My dog Peanut would love you," Wes whispered to Rudy. "He's big and goofy and loves to roll around on the floor, too." Rudy slowly turned over on his back and allowed Wes to pet his stomach.

"That's amazing. I haven't seen Rudy this comfortable with anyone." Ryker couldn't help but smile as his chest flooded with warmth. "You're a dog whisperer, too? What other talents are you hiding?"

"I don't hide. I'm an open book." Wes grinned at Ryker as he slowly sat up.

"A book? Really, Wes? That's cheesy."

"You love cheese—remember, I'm growing on

you, like mold. Moldy cheese."

Ryker rolled his eyes. "I hope your writing is better than your one-liners. Come on, let's visit with the rest of the dogs and cats before we head out."

Rudy unexpectedly clung to Wes's leg and whined when they went to leave, and Ryker's heart melted a bit more for this man.

"I want to have a chat with Charlotte about Rudy before we leave. Can you give me a minute?" Wes asked, so Ryker checked his phone and let Wes have his privacy.

Mac: **Reminder. CALL AT 7** □

Ryker: **Got it. And don't get too excited. Nothing confirmed. Yet.**

Mac: □

Wes finished talking to Charlotte, and then they headed off to grab Thai food on the way back. They wound their way back to Ryker's an hour later.

"Can you find a movie while I plate this up?" Ryker asked from the kitchen as he prepared green tea and got the food unwrapped.

"Anything in particular you feel like watching?" Wes asked as he fiddled with the remote.

"Nah, I'm easy."

"Are you now? Lucky me."

"Funny. Just pick something!"

"Grumpy and bossy. I like it." Wes winked. "Okay, how about *Love Actually?*"

"A rom-com? Really?" Ryker teased.

"Don't be a movie snob. You told me to pick. I picked. We need all the help we can get when it comes to romantic dialogue for our book, so this may be useful research."

They gathered on the sofa, and Spock sat between them, staring at Wes, then Ryker, then back at Wes, hoping that one of the humans would accidentally drop some food or just cave under the canine pressure and hand it over.

"Can't I give him some noodles or something?" Wes asked, petting Spock with one hand. "Look at his face. I can't take these sad eyes and the drool. It's breaking my heart."

"No way. He eats this stuff, he'll either barf or get the runs, and I'm not in the mood to deal with either. Treats are in the large tin on the counter. Go grab him one before you completely give in." Ryker chuckled as Wes hopped up and made his way to the kitchen. "Man, who would've thought you were such a softie?"

"I'm not a softie. I'm hard. All over, baby," Wes said as he flexed his biceps, and Ryker laughed.

"You're too much is what you are. That ego of yours grows by the minute. I'm not sure there's enough space in my apartment to contain it."

"Say what you want about my ego, but you're starting to like me." Wes smiled and Ryker struggled not to reciprocate. Wes was way too appealing for his own good.

They finished eating by seven and set up Ryker's laptop for the video conference. After a few minutes of trying to connect, they noticed that neither the video nor the audio were working. "I'll text Luca. He got this organized with Mac's assistant," Wes offered.

Wes typed furiously on his phone. "Luca wants us to log in again. Should be okay now."

This time, all was good. Mac's face popped up in the top right corner. From the background, it looked like he was still in his office.

"Everything okay now? You can hear me all right?" Ryker asked.

Mac nodded. "Yup, all good. Hey, Wes," he said

as he rubbed his hands through his hair. "Thanks for getting your assistant to set this up. Helena didn't have time before she left. I needed her here until eight, but of course there's always an excuse for why she can't stay late. It may be time to let her go. I can't wait for AI to create a robotic assistant—no excuses, ever!"

"Your assistant obviously has a life outside of work, Big Mac. You might want to take a cue from her unless you're a robot yourself."

Ryker didn't recognize the voice that had spoken, but he noticed that Luca was online as the moderator. Was it him? Did he know he wasn't muted? Shit, Ryker couldn't help but laugh out loud.

"Who the hell said that?" Mac bellowed as Ryker and Wes snickered uncontrollably.

Wes finally calmed down enough to text Luca and advise him to mute himself. Then he showed his phone to Ryker so he could see Luca's response.

Luca: **No, I said what needed to be said. I feel sorry for his assistant. Feel free to use the nickname. LMFAO!**

Luca's twenty-something face popped up on screen. He was striking, with wide chocolate-brown eyes and brown hair with dyed green ends. Definitely someone you wouldn't forget, with his silver nose ring and a swirling, colorful neck tattoo.

"I did. I'm Luca, Wes's assistant." He gave a little wave at everyone. "One hundred percent human and still great at my job, because my boss enjoys work-life balance. I guess in New York you just work until you drop, eh, Macaroni?"

Mac's dark green eyes practically seared them through the screen. "Well, Luca, I believe who I hire or fire is my business. And here in New York, we work hard and we play hard." He paused to sneer. "Anyway, isn't it past your bedtime?"

"Don't worry, old man, I've got energy to spare. I'm heading out for a run once this call is over. Later, Big Mac." Luca got the last word in, closed his video feed, and was now muted.

"Wes, does that man really work for you, or have I been Punk'd?" Mac asked, his face now as red as his hair.

Ryker couldn't ever remember anyone ruffling Mac's calm and professional demeanor like that. Shaking off his laughter, Ryker intervened before Mac totally lost it.

"Okay, okay, moving on, folks," he said. "Wes and I are going to test out this potential partnership over the next few weeks. We'll see if our writing styles mix and let you know our final decision in a month or so."

"Yes! I knew it!" Mac pumped his fist in the air.

"Calm down, Mac. We haven't signed anything yet. This is a trial to see if we can stand working together. I'm still skeptical, and Wes has other opportunities, I'm sure. One month. Okay?"

Mac smiled. "A step in the right direction."

"So, anything else we need to discuss tonight, Big Mac?" Ryker asked with a straight face as Wes laughed out loud.

Mac's middle finger said it all.

Chapter Twelve
Wes

The call ended just after seven thirty PM with no further comedy or drama.

Wes and Ryker talked for almost two hours, enjoying a bottle of Merlot while discussing potential plot lines and upcoming work schedules. They talked about authors they followed, favorite restaurants, and music. Despite Ryker's insistence that he didn't talk much, they hadn't run out of things to say. It was almost like a date but better.

Shit, don't think about the D-word. You hate dating, remember? Wes reminded himself. *Turn your thoughts to something else.*

"Oh, before I forget, here's my homework, Mr. Desoumas, as requested. I e-mailed it to you, but maybe you haven't had a chance to read it yet, so I printed it out. Do I get extra points for writing more than five hundred words?" Wes pulled out a crumpled-up wad of paper and tossed it at Ryker.

"I was kidding about the homework, Wes. I've read your books, so I know the quality of your writing." Ryker opened the paper and silently read and nodded a few times, then finally looked at Wes. "It's good but not great. You're just out of practice."

"I'm really afraid to try my hand at fiction again." He pointed to the paper. "What if I've lost my creative spark? What if good is the only stuff I can churn out now? I want to be great again." Wes sighed and took another sip of wine.

"Every writer should strive to evolve. Mac has been telling me this for the past year, that I need to try something new. So, you're not the only one who feels the pressure. I think you just need quality time to let your imagination unfold. That means less of the party circuit and more creative exercises. Maybe a coach can help, too. Or a writing partner." Ryker paused as Wes raised one eyebrow. "Yes, I see the irony. Anyway. As I was saying, you need less outside noise, more internal focus."

"But what if the focus isn't with me, Master Yoda?" Wes joked, and Ryker laughed, throwing his paper back at him. "Okay, in all seriousness, after the tour, I'll have more time to write. I'll take your advice." Wes paused. "Thanks. It's helpful to talk to someone who knows what I'm going through. Writing can be isolating."

They continued to chat. Ryker selected some music, his eclectic tastes evident in the playlist that echoed softly out of the surround sound speakers—eighties hits, hip-hop, and jazz. As they sat quietly, the sound of John Legend's "All of Me" filled the apartment. Wes felt the energy between them slowly shift from relaxed to sensuous, the blood pulsing through his body like the music, his desire for Ryker growing stronger with every beat. Wes admired Ryker's mellow pose on the couch—his long legs splayed wide, his strong hands rubbing those well-defined thighs. He stared at the line of Ryker's neck as he leaned his head back, his thick, silky hair spread out over the velvet surface of the sofa.

Wes wanted badly to reach out and touch Ryker, but he was afraid to jeopardize the tentative friendship and partnership they'd struck up over the past twenty-four hours. All the stars were now aligned, and Wes was so close to getting what he wanted. Everything except Ryker.

He needed to leave. Now. Before he did something stupid that would ruin everything.

"I'd better go. I've got an early meeting tomorrow with Grey, and then I need to pack for my flight to

Atlanta," Wes said quickly as he rose from the sectional. "Thanks again for a great day. I'm excited to see what the next few weeks bring and whether we can come to an agreement on the book deal. Luca will be in touch with a schedule to get us started."

Wes paused as Ryker stared up at him. The tension between them grew thicker. Ryker finally lifted his head off the sofa and stood up. Taking his glasses off, Ryker sauntered right up to Wes, so close he could see Ryker's pupils dilate, the black becoming ever larger in those big blue depths. Depths Wes could stare into day and night—they were that hypnotically beautiful. The now familiar smells of spice and leather filled his senses, and he watched Ryker's throat move as he swallowed. So much smooth skin to explore. Then Wes's gaze moved south and landed on the large bulge in Ryker's jeans.

Without further thought, Wes reached out and touched Ryker's face, the skin so hot he felt its warmth right down to his toes. Wes enjoyed the contrasting sensation of the rough stubble over smooth cheekbone. Ryker inhaled and closed his eyes, his chest moving in and out, faster and faster.

Wes dove right in. He plunged his hot tongue into Ryker's mouth, tasting wine and Ryker's own spicy essence. Ryker grabbed Wes's ass and pulled him in even closer, crushing their chests together and grinding their denim-covered cocks against one another for more friction.

"Wait, wait," Ryker murmured against his lips, then abruptly pulled away. "What are we doing?"

"I would think that's obvious," Wes replied as he leaned forward and nipped at Ryker's lips. "We have hot fucking chemistry and we want each other. Simple as that."

"Not simple when there's our work partnership to

consider."

Wes sighed and pulled back. Every cell in his body was telling him to take what he wanted and slake the desire that this man ignited inside him. But Ryker wasn't wrong. They were blurring lines, and adding sex to the mix would only make things that much trickier. Unless they agreed to get this out of their system once and for all and then move on with their work endeavor. They could do that. They were both mature enough. Maybe.

Ryker closed his eyes and took several deep breaths, and Wes watched as his body struggled for control.

When Ryker opened his eyes again, Wes could see the answer to the question neither of them wanted to voice.

"Just one night and we'll never think or speak of it again," was all Wes managed to say, and Ryker nodded in agreement. Then Wes wrapped his hand around Ryker's neck and pulled him in for another scorching kiss. Wes felt like he could come just from kissing this man. It was that good. And satisfying this overwhelming desire was well worth any potential fallout.

Ryker moaned and Wes finally came up for air. "Fuck, you taste good," he murmured as he nibbled Ryker's neck. "I'm going to kiss and lick and touch every part of you." Ryker groaned his agreement.

"Don't stop," Ryker whispered urgently.

They stumbled down the hallway to Ryker's bedroom, their shirts littering the floor along the journey. It took a while since they got lost in frantic kisses, but they finally made it to the bedroom, the small bedside lamp casting a warm glow on the dark duvet.

"Have you been tested recently?" Wes asked.

"A month ago. I'm good. My results are in the

bedside drawer," Ryker said between kisses. "You?"

"Two weeks, no one since then. And I'm on PrEP."

"Good."

"Good."

Wes smiled and crushed Ryker's mouth again. Ryker eventually pulled away and dropped to his knees, unzipping Wes's jeans. When Ryker looked up at him, Wes almost lost it.

"Those blue eyes of yours are going to do me in," Wes admitted as he grabbed the base of his cock to calm himself down, staving off his orgasm. He wasn't usually so quick on the trigger. *Fuck, what is this man doing to me?*

His other hand reached out, shaking, and touched Ryker's soft hair, the long strands sliding over his leaking cock and teasing him in the best way. The warm lighting hit Ryker's smooth chest, showing off his defined muscles and supple skin.

Without breaking eye contact, Ryker leaned in. "You'd better brace yourself," he said in a low, husky voice, sticking out his tongue slowly to lick the pre-cum off Wes's cock.

Wes moaned loudly as he looked down, the provocative scene before him even sexier than the one he had conjured up in his hotel shower. Ryker was his dirty fantasy come to life.

Then Ryker rolled his talented tongue around Wes's cock, and Wes knew he was in so much fucking trouble. Lucky him.

****

Ryker

"Fuck, yes, take it all," Wes moaned as Ryker sucked Wes's cock deep into his throat, swallowing the whole length. Wes's cock was uncut and gorgeous, swollen and pulsing. For him. He was salty and musky and tasted so, so good. Ryker loved sucking cock almost as much as he loved receiving it, and he moaned loudly when Wes's earthy taste filled his mouth.

"Jesus, yes! So good, too good," Wes babbled in a hoarse voice, beads of sweat trickling down his cut body.

Ryker took a moment to admire Wes's physique. He was broad, with solid muscles and big biceps, and Ryker wanted those strong arms wrapped around his body. He touched the soft blond hair that scattered over Wes's firm pecs and abdomen and surrounded his big cock. Ryker liked that Wes didn't shave or wax but rather embraced his natural state. Wes's hazel eyes glazed over, so bright they were almost feverish in their intensity. His blond hair was messy, tendrils falling across his forehead, sweat slowly dripping down his face, over his lips. Those lips, so soft and plush, and Jesus, what he could do with them. Shit, Wes was the hottest fucking kiss Ryker had ever experienced.

"Touch yourself," Wes ordered Ryker. "I want to see you come."

Ryker scrambled to unzip his tight jeans, pushing his briefs quickly under his ass to release his long cock, which was aching and flushed. Ryker rubbed his pre-cum over the fat head, then added spit to create a slicker glide. He then leaned back in and drew Wes's cock slowly into his mouth again, licking and sucking hard, until his lips met the base and he could feel Wes's pulsing hardness all the way down his throat.

"Yes. More."

Ryker rubbed his stubbled cheek on Wes's thigh and felt him tremble. He pulled off and took Wes's balls in his mouth one at a time, then trailed his tongue lower to touch Wes's taint. Wes trembled harder. "Keep going."

Ryker moved one hand up, sliding it ever so slowly over Wes's firm ass cheek, then back down the crease. Touching lightly. Teasing. Tormenting.

"Yes, do it," Wes ordered, and Ryker groaned at the encouragement.

Ryker sucked several fingers in his mouth, wetting them real good. He leaned back in and sucked Wes's cock down his throat again while touching his finger to Wes's puckered rim, rubbing and circling, then gently tapping.

"Yes," Wes pleaded, his voice so deep that it reverberated through Ryker's body.

Ryker finally pushed one slippery finger gently into Wes's hot, tight hole. He plunged his finger in and out, fucking him repeatedly while sucking his cock until Wes tapped Ryker's head. "Pull off now if you don't want to swallow my load," he said.

Ryker added a second finger and crooked them, hitting Wes's prostate as Wes cried out his pleasure. "Yes, don't stop!"

Ryker continued to work Wes's tight hole, and it clamped harder around his fingers as Wes's cock twitched in his mouth. With a strangled cry, Wes's orgasm unleashed, and jets of hot, salty cum hit the back of Ryker's throat.

Ryker swallowed all of it and licked Wes clean. He used his other hand to tug at his now painful erection, his gaze roving all over Wes's beautiful body as he stood there gleaming and flushed from his orgasm.

Wes continued to stoke the flames of desire raging inside of Ryker. "That's it, Ry. Come for me, come on me. All over me."

Ryker could come just listening to Wes's hypnotic commands. Standing on shaky legs, he braced himself with one hand on the wall next to Wes's head.

The buildup grew stronger and stronger as Wes continued to urge him on—then total bliss as he jerked once, twice, and shot his load all over Wes.

"*Dios*!" Ryker groaned, cursing as his orgasm went on and on, pulling him under like an immense tidal wave.

Ryker stood there and swayed, his jeans and briefs tangled around his ankles, sweat trickling down his face, his body. He rubbed a soothing hand across his chest, taking in deep gulps of air as his body continued to tremble from the powerful orgasm.

Wes slid a finger through the cum on his abs, then slowly lifted it to his mouth, sticking his tongue out to taste him. "Addictive."

Ry leaned forward and kissed Wes, nipping and tugging at his lower lip to gain entrance. When he finally plunged his tongue inside, he tasted both of them, and what a turn-on that was. He felt his cock stir again, getting ready for round two. Normally, after he came, he was itching to leave his playmate, but in this case, it was way too good to stop. He didn't know if he'd ever get enough. He quickly dismissed that thought and the overwhelming urge to wrap his arms around Wes and never let go.

Ryker reluctantly released Wes's sexy mouth for a moment and looked into his gold eyes, softer now but still glowing.

"One night, remember?" Wes said.

Ryker nodded in agreement. "Then we'd better make the most of it."

Chapter Thirteen
Wes

Wes had a lot of experience with sex.

Hook-ups, threesomes, foursomes, bathroom blowjobs—you name it, he'd enjoyed it. He was, after all, a healthy sexually active man in his thirties. But last night he'd reached a whole other level of satisfaction. Every touch and taste between him and Ryker had been so potent, so electric, he wondered if he'd dreamed it all up. It was better than good. It was the best he'd ever had.

After their first mutual orgasm, they'd shared a steamy shower, and Wes had enjoyed returning the favor by getting on his knees and worshiping Ryker's cock. Then they'd finished up in Ryker's gigantic bed. Wes kept replaying that part in his mind. Probably would for a long time to come.

...Ryker left the shower first, and Wes watched his small but perfect ass flex as he dried himself off. Ryker's back was smooth and sinewy, with a large tattoo of the moon and other planets spread out between his shoulder blades, along with a comet with a blazing tail. He was curious about its meaning but decided to hold off on the questions. He didn't want to break the spell of this one perfect night.

Wes finished drying off and entered the bedroom a few minutes later. His breath hitched at the sight of Ryker lying on his back, legs splayed wide, with his feet flat on the dark duvet.

Ryker's blue eyes glittered in the low light, his smooth chest covered in a fine sheen of sweat, all that long, dark hair spread out over the pillow. Stroking his erect cock with one hand, Ryker had a lubed-up dildo in the other and was moving it in and out of his hole. The sight was so wanton and sexy that Wes wanted to drop to his knees again. Ryker's cock was cut, the large head red and swollen. Wes moaned, recalling how, in the shower, he'd sucked on the head and slid it down to the back of his throat, humming his pleasure and ripping it out of Ryker in a scream so loud he was sure it had woken all the neighbors.

Wes watched Ryker's hand move faster and faster, the toy sliding in and out of his ass as his moans grew louder.

"Come here and fuck me," Ryker said.

How could Wes resist? At this point, he was totally lost to this man, caught in a sensual trance. Wes hurried over to the bed and grabbed the condom and bottle of lube from the nightstand. He quickly suited and lubed up, stroking himself.

"It's my turn now. Give me the toy, Ryker," Wes demanded, his voice deep from the hunger rocking through his body.

Ryker took his time removing the dildo, teasing and taunting Wes. "Like what you see?" he asked with a mischievous smile.

Wes couldn't take any more. He went to his knees in front of Ryker just as Ryker tried to roll over onto his stomach. Normally, Wes didn't care which position he fucked in, but tonight he wanted to see Ryker's deep blue eyes when they reached their climax together. He grabbed Ryker's legs before he could move and hitched them over his shoulders, pulling his ass in the air and entering Ryker in one long, smooth thrust. God, so perfect.

"Just like that. Harder!" Ryker writhed under him and gripped the bedsheets tightly with both hands. "Dios mio, se siente tan bien," he muttered fiercely.

Fuck, just when Wes thought Ryker couldn't get

any sexier, he had to start speaking Spanish and drive Wes out of his mind.

Sweat dripped down Wes's back as he smoothed his hands down Ryker's thighs, massaging the sinewy muscles and taking in every smell, sound, and taste of this moment.

"Ryker, you... I..."

Wes couldn't form any more words after that point. His hips moved faster, thrusting even deeper into Ryker's hole. Wes bent his knees and changed the angle of his hips, his balls slapping Ryker's ass.

"Right there!" Ryker shouted.

Their pace grew frantic. Wes firmly gripped Ryker's cock with one hand, sliding and tugging, determined that his sexy angel would come first. Wes glanced at Ryker's face, and his heart stopped when he saw the raw expression of hunger in those big blue eyes. Suddenly, Ryker's hole spasmed tightly around his dick.

"Wes!"

Wes thrust once more before his vision shattered and he was lost to overwhelming pleasure. Aftershocks rolled through him, and his hips finally slowed their movement. Eventually, he found the strength to open his eyes. He took in Ryker's satiated form, lying there with his arms out, cum all over his stomach and chest, and a smile on his beautiful, swollen lips.

Wes gently pulled out and disposed of the condom, then sauntered back into the bedroom with a warm, wet cloth for Ryker. They cleaned up silently. Wes lay down on the bed, unsure of what to do or say next, if anything. Once again, he was at a loss for words around this man.

Ryker rolled onto his side, head propped up on his hand, and looked down at him with those intense eyes. Wes shivered in reaction. He watched as Ryker leaned in

and kissed him softly, then with increasing urgency.
Would he ever get enough of his tempting mouth? He let
out a sigh, closing his eyes briefly as Ryker continued to
seduce him.

And now it was Tuesday, and Wes was boarding a
plane to Atlanta for his book tour. He should be thrilled.
He'd gotten everything he wanted with none of the day-
after drama. So why was his stomach tied up in knots?

He'd left early in the morning, leaving a note
instead of waking Ryker. Was that a shitty thing to do?
Maybe. But he feared that waking together would only
lead to a repeat of the sexy night they'd shared. And they
had agreed to one night only. It couldn't interfere with
their work. So he'd left without saying goodbye in
person, fighting his inner voice that said don't do it.
They'd expended their mutual passion, and now it was
time to get back to their normal routines. No problem,
since neither of them was looking for anything else.

What else was there? Wes had everything he'd
ever wanted.

He finally got to his seat and settled in, then
stared out the window as the plane taxied down the
runway ten minutes later. Oblivious to his seat mate or
others on board, he let his mind wander to the night
before and wondered why the memory of leaving Ryker
without saying goodbye left him feeling so bereft.

****

Ryker

Ryker woke around ten thirty AM. His bedroom
was dark, and the air was heavy with the lingering smells
of sex and sweat. He reached across the bed to wrap his
arm around Wes, but the only thing he felt was the cold
sheet.

He rubbed his eyes and searched for his glasses, realizing he'd left them in the living room last night—last night, when he'd reached out to Wes and their chemistry ignited in a sensuous dance that blew every other sexual experience he'd had away.

He reached into the bedside drawer for his spare glasses and perched them on his nose, then noticed the paper leaning against a glass of water.

I didn't want to wake you. I don't know what to say. I guess I'm still having writer's block. Or maybe it's just that I'm used to texting and not writing longhand anymore. Probably best I don't say anything about last night except that I had an amazing time.

I'm looking forward to working with you. Text or call anytime.

Wes

P.S. I fed Spock and took him for a walk at seven.

P.P.S. Ship me two dozen Sadie's bagels, pls and thanks.

P.P.P.S. I adopted Rudy from the shelter. Luca is arranging to have him flown up next week and will stay with him until I return from my book tour. Bringing a little bit of New York City home with me.

Ryker smiled at the last item.

"You've got a soft spot, Wes Stewart," he said to himself. "Too bad it's not for me." Though he appreciated the note, Ryker couldn't help but feel slighted that Wes didn't wake him to say goodbye in person. His feelings were ridiculous, really, since they both agreed they would move on after last night.

The apartment was quiet, as per usual. The only sound was that of Spock snoring gently on the dog bed in the corner of the bedroom. Normally, Ryker welcomed the silence, but this morning it felt different. Empty. Lonely even. Funny how having Wes in his space for even a short period of time upended Ryker's routine and left him feeling out of sorts. Wes was a temporary distraction, though, and it was time for Ryker to put this ridiculous sense of disappointment to rest and get back to his usual regimen of work and more work.

Ryker moved his body slowly, stretching out his muscles. He was sore in all the right places. He ran his hand over his puffy lips and glanced down at his skin littered with love bites. His ass felt tender, too, but he'd slept so soundly that he ignored the aches. He'd had a memorable night and he didn't have to deal with any awkward morning-after bullshit. They were both adults who were only interested in physical pleasure. And now that was done, so they could move on. *All is good and normal today. Right?*

Ryker reached out and grabbed the pillow on the other side of the bed, bringing it up to his face. The unique blend of orange, musk, and salt hit him, and he closed his eyes, savoring it. Ryker recalled every sight and sound from last night, but especially the look of pure pleasure that had come over Wes's handsome face when he climaxed.

Shaking himself out of his thoughts, Ryker stripped the bed. He was determined to lock everything from last night—including Wes's lingering scent and euphoric face—in a memory far behind him.

Chapter Fourteen
Wes

Another day, another morning TV show appearance.

Wes loved traveling, but he vowed that this would be the last tour for a good couple of years. He needed time to work on his new project and to unwind.

Good Morning Atlanta was a receptive audience, filled with lots of aspiring writers who were looking for advice to help launch or pivot their creative career. Wes gave a summary of his top five tips for getting published to end off the segment and taping was finalized. Then the lineup for the book-signing part of the event began. Two hours later, he was done.

Wes glanced at the schedule Luca had updated early this morning. After this segment, he had to go to G145 FM for a radio interview, then a break, then a luncheon at the Southern Writers Association. His afternoon was free, with a massage booked at the hotel, and then over to an LGBTQ2S+ benefit at seven PM, where he would sign copies of his latest book and give a brief speech. Hotel overnight and then a flight at nine forty-five AM to Miami. Miami for two days, then fly to New Orleans, etc…

Wes was tired just reading his itinerary. Tired and getting cranky as the morning wore on. He checked his phone, but he still hadn't received a text from Ryker yet, and it was making him fucking antsy. *Is he okay? Pissed off? And why do I care?* He couldn't take waiting any longer.

Wes: **Did you get my note?**

Ryker: **Yup, thanks for taking Spock out. I was able to sleep in for once. And congrats on Rudy. He'll** be a great addition to your family.

Wes: **Thanks, I hope Peanut will be ok with a new brother. Will have to feed them bagels to keep the peace LOL.**

Ryker: **Your bagel wish is my command.**

Wes: **Only bagel wishes?**

What am I doing? Stop it.

Ryker: **Bagels are all I can offer. Have fun in Atlanta.**

Wes: **Will do, take care.**

Ryker: **You too, chat soon.**

Wes shouldn't be disappointed by Ryker's response, but admittedly it stung a bit. What, did he expect Ryker to say one night wasn't enough and they should do it again? *Yes, because it was that good. And not just the sex. I haven't talked and joked with anyone like that in a long time.* Maybe it wasn't the same for Ryker. Wes wasn't normally hung up on what his lovers thought since he usually didn't see them twice. *And now I know why. This line of thinking is pointless. Let it go.*

He texted Grey to see how he was doing. Grey had flown back to Toronto to deal with an office emergency and would guide Wes with any PR stuff as needed via video conference for the rest of his tour. Wes hoped he was going to take some time to rest and reminded himself to ask about the mystery man leaving Grey's hotel room in New York City. Grey had been too quiet the morning he left, and Wes prayed that everything was okay.

Finally, he called Luca.

"Hey, bossman. How's it going?" Luca asked, upbeat as usual.

"Good. The TV segment this morning went well, and there were lots of great audience questions. I'm just about to head off for the radio interview, so thought I'd call and catch up."

There was a silent pause until Luca spoke again. "Mac Duran is the most uptight pain in the ass I've had the displeasure of working with. He sent a draft agreement in the hopes that you and Ryker will make it official. Then he called me twice to make sure I got it even though I sent a receipt e-mail to confirm. And he e-mailed me again. Then he called me again. That man needs a vacation and a good fuck, and not necessarily in that order."

Wes couldn't help but laugh at Luca's observation. "Please tell me you didn't give him that advice?"

"No, but I hinted that all work and no play makes for a very grumpy and stressed-out gay. He hung up on me."

Wes laughed, heading outside and glancing around for his car service. "Man, I wish I had been there to see Mac's face. You really push his buttons."

A black Mercedes pulled up to the curb, and the front window rolled down. "Mr. Stewart?" the young driver said. Wes nodded. "Good day to you, sir. I'm Hayden and I'll be your driver for the remainder of the day." He leapt out of the car and opened the back door for Wes.

"I don't want to go anywhere near Big Mac's buttons. He irks me with that icy attitude of his," Luca said. "Anyway, enough talk about *that* man. Did you read the notes I sent for the benefit tonight? You'll be at the head table with the mayor and Ashton Langley, the founder and CEO of PrideAtlanta. I sent you his bio and pic. Short dark hair, green eyes, dimples." Luca sighed. "You are one lucky man, Wes Stewart."

"Thanks, Luca. I'll text if I have last-minute questions. Later."

"Good luck!"

And with that, Wes ended the call. He nodded at the driver and slid into the backseat.

While the car whizzed through the busy streets of Atlanta, Wes opened the e-mail Luca had sent and reread it, familiarizing himself with the names and faces registered to attend. Besides the mayor and his wife, there would be some bigwig from the media and a few local celebrities at the head table.

He clicked on Ashton Langley's photo and read his bio. Forty-five years old. Widower. His husband had passed away six years ago from cancer. One adopted son, age eleven. A venture capitalist and successful business owner, he'd started the charity in memory of his husband, and it was now his primary focus. Ashton was a strong advocate in a region that still struggled with acceptance of the LQBTQ2S+ community. Wes was impressed and looked forward to meeting him.

He glanced at the photo again. Luca was right—Ashton was a very good-looking man.

Too bad he wasn't a cranky New Yorker.

****

Ryker

Revisions, revisions, and more revisions. After four hours at his laptop, Ryker finally took a break and went for a walk with Spock, the warm spring air and sunny skies lifting his mood. He tried not to think about Wes, but that was futile. They were testing their writing partnership and would be corresponding a lot, especially if they signed an agreement, so naturally, Ryker would be thinking about him. Them. Together.

No, not them together. Working together. Work only.

Ryker just needed to avoid flirting with Wes,

though that could be a tall order. Wes was a natural tease, so it was bound to happen occasionally. Unless Wes had other distractions to keep him happy. Ryker winced at that thought. He did not want to think about Wes fucking other men.

Shit. I never do this with any of my other hook-ups. What the hell is wrong with me?

Searching for a distraction, Ryker decided to check out Grindr to see if there was anyone nearby looking for a little playtime this week. He needed a release with a new man. Then he could get back to his usual self.

Ryker headed back home, wrote for another two hours, then searched the kitchen cupboards for something to snack on. He texted Javier, and they agreed to meet at the Gambit pub in a few days to discuss the benefit for the shelter. Ryker was still determined to make a donation in place of attending, but he didn't want to offend Javier and preferred to tell him in person. Plus, Ryker decided to meet a guy later that night at the same pub. Life was back to normal.

He checked his phone again, but there were no further texts from Wes. Rationally, Ryker knew it was a good thing, but his chest still tightened a bit in disappointment. He shook it off. Wes's schedule for the next few weeks was insane, so Ryker would let him reach out when he had time.

Ryker made his daily call to Cal to see if he'd had any further texts from his anonymous creeper.

"Hey, bud, how are you? Any more messages this week?" Ryker asked, grabbing a cracker to munch.

"Nope, all quiet, thank God! Hopefully, that's the end of it. Now on to some good news. Mac told me you and Wes are working together. Congrats, man."

"It's not a done deal yet," Ryker mumbled and

shoved another cracker in his mouth.

"That's not what Mac seems to think. Anyway, I think working with someone else will be good for you, you know, shake up your creative juices. Though you might have a hard time concentrating since Wes is quite the distraction. Funny, good-looking, and that deep voice, hmmm, fuck me," Cal said with a chuckle.

Ryker inhaled too quickly, and he coughed as cracker crumbs hit his throat. He exhaled, then took another deep breath to gather himself. A vision of Wes from last night flashed through his mind. *Fuck me*, indeed. Funny how talking about Wes made him nervous now instead of irritated.

"Yeah." He coughed. "We'll see. He's actually a pretty decent guy so far. We chatted Monday night over wine at my place, and we're going to see how the next few weeks unfold. A test period before we sign. Did I mention he came over to my place before he left? Yeah, he met my mom and then came with me to the shelter and adopted Rudy, you know, the dog we rescued a month ago? My cats love him, too, which is odd. And then he took Spock for a walk Tuesday before he left, and…" Ryker's babbling came to an abrupt stop when he realized his mistake.

"Wait. Rewind, my friend. He was over on Monday night and then he was there Tuesday morning? Well, well, well, you naughty boy. Did you two fuck? You did, didn't you?" he teased Ryker.

Ryker's face heated at the thought of Wes, memories of their night together resurfacing despite his best attempts to forget.

"Yes, okay? We fucked. We spent hours in various sexual positions. It was fucking awesome sex and now it's over. Neither of us are into relationships, so it all works out. With that out of our systems, we can focus on writing. We're on good terms. We understand each other. No worries." Christ, he was babbling again.

"Mmm, yeah, I don't know if I buy that, Ry. I think there's more going on here than a quick roll in the sheets. You met him at Mac's and gave him the evil eye. Then he charmed you. Twenty-four hours later, you're introducing him to your mother. He adopts one of the dogs you rescued, and you celebrate your 'soon-to-be partnership' with wine, music, and a night of fucking? You know what? I smell a Hallmark movie! Ooooooh, Ry's in looove," Cal sang out.

Ryker rolled his eyes and ran a hand through his tangled hair.

"Gimme a break, *Callum*. Mom came by to interrogate him, and the dog adoption was just the right place, the right time. Wes and I fucked. That's it. Now he's on his tour, probably off having sex with a different man every night of the week." Ryker's stomach clenched. "And I'll hook up with someone else when I have time, and that's that. I feel nothing. No feelings of any kind. No feelings. Except nice ones—friendly, good feelings. But not *that* kind of good. More like warm, but not *that* kind of warm. Nope." Ryker shut up as he flushed and paced the floor. Shit. Incoherent much?

Cal was silent for a moment. "You know, I've never heard you talk so much on one phone call. Like, ever. You're normally 'hi, how are you, bye.' Something is up with you and your reaction to Wes. You know, it's okay to have feelings."

Ryker laughed out loud. "This from a man who has never had an intimate relationship that lasted longer than an hour. What do you know about love, Cal?"

"I said feelings. You said love."

Ryker paused his pacing and suddenly felt lightheaded, like he was going to pass out. *It's just hunger. Eat another cracker.*

"And I don't know any more about feelings than you do, my friend, but I know you're behaving differently and it's all to do with Wes. Anyway, I'm glad you had a good time. And that you two are okay to test out your work partnership now that you've seen each other's naked bits." Cal cackled.

Ryker took a deep breath and pressed his fingers to his eyes. "Don't say naked bits. Jesus! And what about you? Didn't you go home with someone, or several someones, after you left the club on Saturday night?"

"Who told you that? There was no one. Nothing happened!" Cal said vehemently. "Hey, someone's at the door. Gotta go!"

And with that, Ryker was left staring at his phone in confusion. Spock let out a whine and ducked his tiny head into the sofa cushions.

"What?" he asked his dog, as Spock continued to hide.

Ryker was glad he wasn't the only one acting weird today.

Chapter Fifteen
Wes

A slim-fit tuxedo on a muggy Southern evening was a very bad idea.

Wes had probably sweated off five pounds waiting outside his hotel for Hayden to drive him to the Marshall Hotel, the venue for tonight's benefit. Located in southeast Atlanta, the hotel was a historic landmark from the 1920s, and tonight the rooftop bar would host the who's who of Atlanta for cocktail hour. Wes reviewed the notes Luca had sent for one last prep, but his eyes kept straying to his phone and, in particular, his last text message thread with Ryker.

He quickly snapped a selfie and sent it to Ryker.

Wes: Note to self, tuxedos and warm weather do not mix. This suit is now permanently glued to my body.

Wes noted the now familiar black sedan pulling up in front of the hotel.

"Looking sharp tonight, Mr. Stewart," Hayden commented as he exited the vehicle and opened the back door for Wes.

"Thanks, Hayden, but I can't wait to get into air conditioning. This suit is too warm for this weather," he replied as he slid into the cool comfort of the car.

It took only ten minutes to arrive at the venue, and he was once again hit by the wall of humidity when the car door opened.

"Have a nice evening, Mr. Stewart. Send me a text when you're ready to head back," Hayden replied, and was off.

Wes entered the hotel through the wide double doors and headed to the elevator that would take him up to the rooftop bar. A short while later, he emerged on the twentieth floor and was greeted by Shelby Goffen, the event planner. Dressed in a green sateen cocktail dress, her fiery red curls bouncing on her shoulders, Shelby was an energetic sight. She was organized and friendly, with perfect Southern manners.

"Wes, so nice to meet you! Welcome to Atlanta. Would you care for a drink?" she asked, motioning for a waiter. Wes ordered a champagne cocktail. "Oh, I have the set-up here with copies of your books for you to sign. I sent the updated list of guests at the head table to you and Luca."

"Thanks, Shelby, this is great. Luca sends his best, by the way. He really enjoyed talking to you last week."

"He's amazing, a real pleasure to work with. I told him to call me anytime. I'm happy to offer any guidance he may need to launch his event business. Oh, here's my assistant, Rochelle Hetter." Shelby motioned to a young woman with long, dark hair and vivid makeup, wearing a retro-style polka dot dress.

"Nice to meet you, Mr. Stewart," Rochelle said and shook Wes's hand.

"Please call me Wes," he replied.

Shelby smiled at the two of them. "Rochelle will be your shadow tonight, so anything you need, ask her. Is there anything else I can do? I have a few items I need to take care of in the grand ballroom before everyone heads there for dinner," she said as her phone pinged.

"I'm good. I'll see you later."

And with that, Shelby was on her phone and rushing off to the elevator.

Wes's phone buzzed. "Excuse me for a moment, Rochelle," he said.

Ryker: **You couldn't pay me to wear that. But**

it suits you, **Prince Charming.**

Wes couldn't help but smile and quickly typed a response.

Wes: **I wouldn't want to disappoint the 300 guests tonight. They expect only the best.**

Ryker: □ **Too bad you have no self-confidence. 300 people? I'm sweating for you. I'm already anxious just thinking about attending the shelter benefit next month.**

Wes's smile faded as he thought of Javier's attempts to get closer to Ryker. Had the man convinced Ryker to go with him to the event as his date? Wes's gut churned at that thought.

Wes: **You decided to go? What changed your mind?**

Ryker: **Meeting Javier to discuss. Haven't decided yet but I feel like I should go, force myself to be social. Someone I met recently has made me realize that I should take a few more chances in life.** □

Wes's stomach continued to roll, both in pleasure at Ryker's last comment and in unease at Ryker's meetup with Javier. He took a deep breath and then a long sip of his drink.

Rochelle's smooth voice interrupted his thoughts. "Wes, we need you inside for introductions and photos. If you'll step this way, please." She motioned to the doorway.

Wes: **Time to greet the fans, TTYL.**

Wes decided it was best to forget about Ryker for the rest of the night and focus on the evening ahead. No good would come of texting and flirting with him anyway. *Focus on work.*

Rochelle led him through the large crowd to a small group gathered near the long, mahogany bar, and Wes recognized Ashton Langley immediately. He was handsome, as per his picture: about Wes's height and build, with dark green eyes and a close-trimmed beard that was classic and stylish. Ashton was talking to the mayor and, presumably, his wife.

Rochelle made the introductions. "The Honorable Mayor Jesse Linton, Mrs. Amelia Linton, and PrideAtlanta CEO Ashton Langley, may I introduce you to one of our esteemed guests this evening? International best-selling author Wesley Stewart from Toronto, Canada. Mr. Stewart is a well-known fiction and non-fiction author who has kindly donated books for tonight's benefit and is our keynote speaker."

The usual small talk was made, and more cocktails appeared. Mayor Linton was a heavyset man in his late fifties, with a permanent smile showcasing very large teeth. He reminded Wes of a pushy car salesman—fitting, given his job. Mrs. Linton was a petite woman, polite but rather quiet for a politician's wife. Then again, the mayor hardly let her get a word in. They chatted about local events and history, and Wes started to relax and enjoy the evening until the mayor cornered him.

"You know, Wesley," the mayor said as he placed a hand on Wes's shoulder. "My son is interested in writing. He volunteers at the student newspaper at college. Maybe you could have a chat with him. Or meet up with him since you're in town. I could…"

"Mayor Linton," Ashton interrupted, "Wesley is a guest tonight, and he has a very busy schedule." He then paused dramatically. "Look, isn't that Chase Declair over by the lounge? He's Atlanta's top news anchor." He pointed to a handsome blond man dressed in a sharp navy tuxedo.

"Why, yes, yes, it is. Well, Wesley, it was so nice chatting with you. I have some circulating to do. See y'all later." And with that, the mayor quickly scuttled away with his wife in tow, pushing his way through the crowd to get to the reporter.

"That man will do anything to feed his agenda to the media." Ashton laughed, sipping his drink and shaking his head. "Anyway, Wes, I want to thank you again for coming tonight. This fundraiser is key to PrideAtlanta's success, and we are honored to have you here. It's so important for LGBTQ youth to have positive roles models." He motioned to the bar stools, and they sat.

"It's my pleasure. I'm proud to support initiatives like this. Anything I can do to foster equality, I'm in." Wes paused and looked around the rooftop, admiring the view of the city skyline. "So tell me, Ashton, what's all the fuss over the news anchor?"

Ashton's posture became rigid as he glanced at Chase, who had been cornered by the mayor. "Chase started out as an investigative journalist. He's very well respected. We went to the same college, so he's an old acquaintance. After graduating, he worked in Miami before returning here two years ago. Now he anchors the local news and is very popular. Would you like to meet him?"

Ashton ran a hand over his tie, then loosened the knot at his neck. "I spoke too soon. He managed to slip away from the mayor, and he's headed this way."

The crowd parted as Chase sauntered over. "Good evening. I'm Chase Declair. And you are the novelist Wesley Stewart. It's an absolute pleasure to have an author of your caliber visit our humble city," Chase said with a big smile, and Wes could see why so many people had turned their heads as he walked through the crowd.

"Thank you. Wes, please. It's nice to meet you as well, Chase."

"Ash, nice to see you again." Chase's smooth

voice iced over as he glared at Ashton. "Keeping all the handsome men to yourself, as usual, I see."

The two men stared at each other in a tense stand-off, and Wes suddenly felt like an interloper. The blistering look they shared went on so long that Wes decided to break the awkward tension.

"Rochelle just texted," he said. "Dinner is ready. Shall we head on down?" Wes motioned to Ashton and Chase.

"I need another drink, but y'all go on ahead. Oh, and be sure to save me a dance, Wes," Chase said as he winked and sauntered away.

"What an infuriating, irritating pain in the ass," Ashton grumbled as they headed down to the ballroom.

"Bad history?" Wes asked, very curious about the simmering animosity between Ashton and Chase. This evening was turning out to be far more interesting than he'd imagined.

"About a decade ago, he wrote a national piece about judicial corruption and called out my late father, who was a circuit court judge. Chase was an investigative reporter at the *Miami Journal* at the time. You know, uncovering the secrets of people in power, showing their true colors and their hypocrisy. It painted a rather unfortunate picture of my father's personal and professional failings, and I was furious. Chase insisted it was backed by research, sources. It turned out that much of what he'd written was true, but it still hurt, especially the personal revelations. And now, whenever we see each other at these things, the anger boils over. I know he was just doing his job, but he seems to take delight in saying I told you so. He's always so smug. Most people think he's a Southern charm—intelligent, funny, and gorgeous, but I just want to wipe that perfect smile right off his face."

A dark stain of red bloomed over Ashton's

cheeks, and he loosened his tie again. "I'm sorry, Wes. You don't need to witness our drama show. Let's go grab our seats."

Three hours and several speeches later, the party finally got started. The live band was high energy, amping up the audience, and everyone was having a good time. It was amazing to see so many LGBTQ2S members and supporters, and Wes was impressed by the youth that were leading the way for change. Wes also enjoyed chatting with Ashton at dinner, but he didn't feel any spark, even though he was a very attractive man. In fact, he hadn't really felt anything all night, despite several flirtatious glances from a few men. He checked his phone again but noticed no new texts from his grumpy partner. Writing partner, that is. A rush of disappointment moved through him until he reminded himself that mooning over Ryker would get him nowhere.

A smooth voice teased Wes's ear. "May I have this dance?"

Wes turned and found himself up close to Chase, who held out his hand expectantly. Wes glanced at Ashton, whose face tightened, along with his grip on the crystal wineglass, his knuckles turning white. Ashton quickly turned away to talk to the female guest on his right.

"Why not? But I lead," Wes joked as they made their way to the dance floor.

The band was performing a slow, soulful rendition of Lady A's "Need You Now." Wes and Chase started to sway to the music together.

"Smile!"

Wes turned at that announcement, and a bright flash flooded his eyes. He recognized the photographer of the evening, who nodded his head.

"Nice one. Thanks, gentlemen," he said before

moving on to capture other couples and singles.

"I hope I get a copy of that picture, or no one will believe I danced with *the* Wes Stewart." Chase chuckled. "I really enjoyed your speech tonight. Very few people can speak without reading the whole thing from their notes. I imagine you get a lot of public appearance requests," Chase said with a smile.

"I do, but I'm getting more selective. I really love events like this one and the ability to use my public position for positive change." He paused. "And what about you, Chase? Do you enjoy your work?"

"Immensely. I appreciate being back in my hometown, too. There's something about this city and this state that just won't let go of me." Chase turned his head and nodded at the mayor dancing nearby with his wife. "And the weather ain't bad either. It's great if you're like me and you need to stay active year-round. I loved Miami, but the summers just killed me. What about you? Do you enjoy living in Toronto?"

"I do. It's a multicultural city with lots of good restaurants, parks, and festivals. A bit like New York but less frenetic. But I'm on the road a lot, too. I love to travel for pleasure, and I'm looking forward to some of that once my book tour is done."

"Maybe you can head on down here another time for pleasure instead of business," Chase joked.

Wes smiled politely. Despite the close contact, Wes's body wasn't reacting to Chase. Not like it reacted to Ryker. Did Ryker dance? Wes certainly hoped so. His body had moved so fluidly when they were in bed together.

"Earth to Wes," Chase murmured, his large hands running up Wes's back.

"Sorry, Chase. Just tired and caught up in my head."

Chase laughed, a twinkle in his blue eyes. "And here I was hoping to invite you back to my place for a nightcap."

"Thanks for the offer, but I'm wiped out," Wes replied.

Chase grinned at Wes. "Is that all? Got someone else on your mind?"

"Yes," Wes said automatically. "Wait, no." He shook his head. "No. I'm just tired."

As the dance finished, Wes decided the best way to shake his weird mood was to focus on someone else and play matchmaker. "I think there's another man you should talk to tonight and maybe invite for a nightcap," he said as he waved Ashton over.

Chase shook his head. "No way. You don't understand, Wes. It's complicated. Ash and I have a long history. I did this piece on his father, and he refuses to acknowledge that I did the right thing in exposing the man for the crook he was, far from the saint he portrayed. Ashton Langley may have been voted one of Atlanta's most eligible gay men, but he is a stubborn, hot-tempered control freak. Every time I see him, I just want to grab him and tell him to wake up."

Wes held up a hand. "Have a real conversation with him and bury your long-standing feud, and maybe skip the personal jabs. He may or may not want to hear what you have to say, but you've got nothing to lose."

Ashton walked up to them, his dark brows furrowed in irritation.

Wes sighed. "I'm beat, so I'm going to head back to my hotel. Chase, thanks for the dance. It was very nice to meet you. And, Ashton, I had a great evening. Best of luck with your ongoing work. I'm happy to support PrideAtlanta however I can," he said, shaking Ashton's hand. "Here's my number and e-mail. Let's keep in touch." He then handed over his personal cards to both men.

"Thank you again for being here tonight," Ashton replied and made to turn away until Wes stopped him. "Ashton, Chase needs to talk to you."

And with that, Wes left the ballroom, though he stopped at the door to see how his little maneuver had unfolded. Chase reached out and touched Ashton's arm, leaning over to whisper in his ear. He then placed a hand on Ashton's hip and drew him back onto the dance floor. Ashton looked stiff and uncomfortable, but he went along with it, and they started talking as they swayed slowly to the music. No raised voices or angry faces. So far, so good.

Wes observed the intense way they reacted to each other. Chemistry like that could not be denied.

He should know. *Ryker.*

Chapter Sixteen
Ryker

Ryker was unusually grumpy by week's end.

Even his fur babies ignored him. He was terse with his editor and lambasted his agent. Then he called back to apologize to both of them. He couldn't seem to get into a regular sleep pattern, and his anxiety grabbed hold of him once again. And last night, he'd had a nightmare—a bad one.

The rest of the week, he'd woken in the middle of the night and just couldn't fall back asleep. He'd tried to distract himself by working long hours finalizing his current book. Meanwhile, Wes had traveled to Miami and then New Orleans, texting about his travels and sending ideas and suggestions for their collaboration. Ryker reviewed Wes's notes and decided that they should formalize their partnership and get an agreement done up. It was time to get off the fence and commit. Ryker should've been happy. He was starting a new venture that would hopefully mean bigger things for his career. Instead, he was irritable and frustrated.

Ryker kept his communications with Wes focused on work even though he'd been tempted to ask about his latest social media posts. He'd seen a picture of Wes at the PrideAtlanta benefit, dancing with a very good-looking man named Chase Declair. Ryker had Googled the name and found out he was the head anchor at the *Atlanta Evening Edition*. In the picture, Declair had his arms around Wes, and Wes was smiling at the camera as if he were on top of the world. Which he should be, Ryker supposed, since it appeared he had men falling over him everywhere he went.

Not that it's any of my business, Ryker repeated to

himself for the tenth time.

Then there was another picture of him with Ashton Langley, the CEO of PrideAtlanta. They were sitting together at dinner, laughing and drinking wine.

Only a week ago that was me, laughing and drinking wine with Wes. And then we kissed.

Ryker's phone pinged, and he glanced down hopefully. When he saw Javier's name, his mood soured again. He missed Wes's fun and flirty texts. Stupid. Admonishing himself for such ridiculous behavior, he willfully ignored his heart's truth. He rubbed his chest absently in the hopes of making the strange ache in it go away. Feeling this needy and wanting was fucking with his head. He needed a diversion.

Javier: **Hey, we still on for tonight at 5:30?**

Ryker: **Yup, meet you at the Gambit. I'll grab a booth near the back of the bar.**

Javier: **Sounds perfect, can't wait.**

Good thing he was going to get some much-needed relief tonight. He'd agreed to meet up with a man named Henry at the same pub around eight. He would get his mind off Wes and focused on someone else. A good sexual release, and all would be right again in Ryker's world.

A quick shower later, Ryker changed into dark jeans and a plain black t-shirt. He decided to leave his hair in a ponytail, then added eyeliner.

Before he left, he made one important phone call. It went to voicemail.

"Hey, Cal, it's me. Just checking to see if you're okay. Call or text me when you get this, doesn't matter what time. Later, bud."

After taking Spock for a walk, he fed the fur babies and was on his way. He arrived at the pub early and grabbed the last booth at the back, motioning to the waitress.

"Hey, I'll have a pint of the Devil's Kiss and two food menus, please," he said.

"Sure thing," she replied.

Ryker waved when he saw Javier enter, dressed up in slacks and a nice button-down. They both ordered the bacon cheeseburger and fries, then chatted for a bit about the latest rescues at the shelter and the upcoming benefit.

Ryker leaned forward. "Look, I know you mean well, but large events are not my thing. I get anxious in big crowds, and small talk with strangers is like tiny talk to me. Just thinking about it is making me twitch."

Javier smiled and reached out to touch Ryker's hand. "But everyone from the shelter will be there. It won't be like you're with total strangers. As your date, I'd be there with you."

Ryker interrupted. "Javier, you seem like a great guy, but I'm not interested in you that way. I like you, as a friend, but that's it. I don't do romantic relationships. Trust me, you're better off. I've got baggage you don't want to open." Ryker pulled his hand away and rubbed his bracelets.

Javier shook his head. "Everyone has baggage, Ry. You know, we could just hook up, keep it casual."

"That's not what you're looking for. If it was, you'd have suggested it the first time we met." Ryker paused and let out a big sigh.

Javier nodded. "True. Well, I still hope you'll attend the event. We'd love to have you there."

"I'll think about it and let you know." Ryker rubbed his hand over his face.

"Are you okay?"

"I'm not sleeping well this week."

"You mean since Wes left?"

"Yes. I mean, no!" Ryker paused and took a deep breath. "Yes, since then, but not because of Wes leaving. Insomnia is common for me. It's been a stressful week," Ryker babbled, his face flushed.

"I see." Javier smiled slowly. "Well, I'm going to take off. How much do I owe you?"

Ryker waved him off, picking up the bill. "I've got it."

"Thanks for dinner. I'll see you next Monday, per usual."

Ryker nodded. "Have a good night, Javier."

Half an hour later, Ryker was sipping his second beer, waiting for Henry. *Ping!*

Wes: **You have time to chat?**

Perfect fucking timing. Not. The last thing Ryker needed was Wes on his mind when his hook-up was due to arrive.

Ryker: **No**

Wes: **K**

Ryker inhaled quickly. *Don't be a dick,* he admonished himself.

Ryker: **Sorry, bad week. What's up?**

Wes: **Nothing that can't wait.**

Ryker: **Tomorrow?**

Wes: **Sure, take care.**

Ryker: **You too.**

"Ryker?" A strange voice called out his name. Ryker looked up to find a slim man in his twenties staring down at him. "Henry," the man said, taking a seat across from him.

Ryker was surprised by two things: one, how cute Henry was in real life, with his dark curly hair and big grin; and two, the fact that Ryker had no physical reaction to him. At all. It was like Ryker's cock was the only part of him now capable of sleep. *Wake up!*

Henry ordered a drink, and they sat quietly, throwing out a couple of awkward questions and answers here and there. But Ryker was struggling to find words now that his sex drive had decided to go on vacation.

"Look, I have to get going." Ryker stood up and placed a couple of twenties on the table. "Sorry for wasting your time."

Henry smiled and looked around. "Not a waste. You paid for my drink, and I'm sitting in a bar with lots of potential for the evening."

He extended his hand and Ryker shook it. Nada.

"Have a good night, Henry," he said.

Ryker entered his apartment at eight thirty when Cal called back.

"Hey, bud. Everything okay?" Ryker asked.

"All's good. No more weird texts, so I'm relieved. Sorry I missed your call. I just got caught up working on a new piece. Oh, and I have some interesting ideas for the book cover for *1,000 Days*. I'll send you my samples next week."

"Cool. I'm headed to bed."

"It's eight thirty! Is your insomnia worse again? Wait, maybe you're lovesick," Cal teased.

"No. And knock it off. I'm just not sleeping well. You know, with work stress."

"You miss having a warm, handsome Canadian author in your bed, don't you?" Cal laughed.

"I'm hanging up now," Ryker said, and did so.

He shook his head, grabbing the TV remote. He searched for a movie to help him relax before going to bed.

His phone rang again a minute later.

"I told you, Cal, I'm not lovesick. I'm tired."

There was silence before a familiar voice chuckled. "Well, hello, Sleeping Beauty. Or should I say

Sleepy Beauty? So, you miss me, huh? I knew you couldn't resist the lure of my magnificent being." Wes's deep laugh echoed on the phone, warming Ryker from the inside out and doubling his heart rate. *Check before you answer, idiot!*

"I'm rolling my eyes right now. You really are the most ridiculous, egotistical man I have ever met. Seriously, Wes, I think you need a larger body to hold up your big head."

"But you like my big head, baby," Wes teased.

"*Baby*? Have you been drinking tonight? Wait, why are you calling me?"

"Your text said you had a bad week. I wanted to be sure you were okay. And, yes, I've been drinking just a wee bit. New Orleans is wild, Ry. I attended a writers' conference today, and they had free drinks flowing all fucking day. By the time five PM rolled around, I needed to go back to my room to take a nap. And now I'm headed out again for the closing dinner." Wes paused and lowered his voice. "But enough about me. Why did you have a bad week? Are you sleeping okay?"

No, because you're not beside me. That was the first thought that entered Ryker's head, even though he didn't say it out loud. Couldn't, when he didn't even know how to process it. Spock must've sensed Ryker's distress; he bounded up onto the couch beside him, throwing his small, furry body over Ryker's lap and cuddling close. Ryker hugged Spock for comfort before he could speak again.

Wes must've put a spell on him or something, because the last time Ryker had slept soundly was the night they spent together.

"It doesn't really matter. Besides, I told you I've been busy."

"I know that, but I'm worried about you."

"Wes, the social butterfly, managed to find time between events to worry about little old me?" Ryker teased.

Wes hesitated in his reply. "You're my writing partner now, so I have a vested interest. We need to be honest with each other if this collaboration is going to work."

Ryker sighed. "I told you I was a journalist, right?" Ryker paused. "Wait, do you have time for this? I thought you had to leave."

"I'm not making a speech. I can be there whenever. Let's use FaceTime instead." They switched, and Ryker could now see Wes's gorgeous face and the hotel room beyond. "You were saying?"

"Sometimes I have nightmares. It all goes back to when I was a naive twenty-five-year-old reporter. I was partnered with a senior writer to do a story on a serial killer from Brooklyn. You've heard of the Dollhouse Murders?"

Ry paused and Wes nodded, his brow creased in concern.

"Several young people in their twenties were raped and killed," Ryker went on. "The killer posed their corpses with a doll cradled in their arms. Anyway, when they arrested the killer, everyone was vying for an opportunity to interview him. We got our chance. The killer took a liking to me—I guess due to my age and similarity to his male victims—and insisted that I be the one to interview him. I visited him several times in jail, but by the third time, I'd had enough. He was just toying with me. He didn't give me any real information that I could use for our story. My colleague kept pushing me to go back. I refused." Ryker paused again.

"The killer escaped when they were transferring him to the courtroom for his bail hearing. He showed up outside my office when I was leaving late one night. Guess he had access to the Web to search out where I worked. I often headed out the back exit in the alleyway, and he was waiting there. And he… He grabbed me and punched me, knocked me out cold, and apparently started to drag my body away until another colleague exited the building and scared him off. I was in the hospital for two days with a concussion."

"Jesus, Ry. I don't know what to say. Fuck, I'm so sorry."

Ryker nodded and continued, "When I was released from the hospital, I withdrew from everything. I quit my job. I couldn't leave my apartment because I was so scared. They finally caught him a few months later, but by that time I was already a mess. Finally, my mom and my friends got me to a doctor, and I gradually got better. Medication, therapy, self-defense classes, I did it all. And I discovered creative writing. Mac was instrumental in encouraging me. At first it was an escape, but it was also very healing. It gave me purpose again. I've made a good life for myself, but sometimes, despite my best efforts, the nightmares come back." Ryker gave a huge sigh as he finished.

"I wish there was something I could say to make things better. Can I ask what happened to the man that assaulted you?"

"He was eventually tried and convicted of first-degree murder of four of his eleven victims. They dropped the assault charges from his plea deal, but he was still sentenced to life. I don't worry about him coming after me anymore like I did years ago, but when I get stressed or anxious, the nightmares resurface. It's the same type of scenario where I'm usually trying to get away from him, but I'm trapped. Talking about it helps. I only had one nightmare this week. Just between you and me, Cal recently had an anonymous person sending him weird text messages. I've been worried about him, so I think that might have triggered it. The rest of this week I just kept waking up at two or three in the morning. I start thinking about stuff and can't get back to sleep."

"I didn't have nightmares after my parents passed, but I did have insomnia. I couldn't fall asleep at all, and my grandmother tried everything. Therapy helped a lot and time. We all deal with grief and trauma in our own way. Just remember to reach out to people when you need it."

Wes was lying back on the hotel bed, running a hand through his hair. He shifted the phone in his hand, and those warm hazel eyes locked onto Ryker's. "Don't freak out on me when I say this." He paused. "I wish I was there with you to give you a hug."

Ryker smiled. "Don't freak out on me either, but I wish you were here, too."

"What's happening with us?" Wes asked, rubbing a hand over his jaw, his lips.

"I don't know, but it's fucking scary," Ryker said truthfully.

Ryker's mind wandered back to those pictures of Wes in Atlanta, dancing with a handsome man. Was Wes being truthful about wanting to be with him? These deeper feelings were overwhelming for someone who only had casual relationships, and Ryker couldn't help but worry about what it all meant. Would they be able to keep their work and personal feelings separate, or were they creating a situation that was destined to come to a messy and complicated ending?

There was a loud banging sound in the background, and Wes turned his head. "Shit, that's my fellow writers come to drag me out to dinner. I gotta go, but call me later if you need to talk, okay?"

Ryker nodded and Spock raised his head, sniffing at the phone. "Spock, no, do not lick the phone!" Ryker said.

Wes laughed. "I'm glad Spock is there for you." Spock barked at Wes's voice and continued to lick the phone. "Hey, Spock, give your daddy a kiss for me and make him feel better," Wes said. And with that, he gave a wave. Then the screen went blank.

Ryker leaned his head back and closed his eyes. Wes's face and voice reverberated in his mind so clearly that he finally, happily, drifted off to sleep.

Chapter Seventeen
Wes

While everyone around him at the annual NOLA Writers' Association dinner partied like it was 1999, Wes spent the evening thinking about Ryker. He needed to hear his voice again. Faking a headache, Wes excused himself from the festivities just after midnight and grabbed a rideshare back to the Willow Hotel.

Wes threw off his jacket and undid his tie. He sat down on the bed, unbuttoned his shirt, and unzipped his pants, making himself comfortable. He debated calling Ryker back—would he wake him? He opted to text instead.

Wes: **R u up?**

Ryker: **I am now.**

Wes: **Shit, sorry. Go back to sleep**

Ryker: **Nah, kidding. I drifted off for a few hours and woke up ten minutes ago.**

Wes: **Can I call?**

Ryker: **FaceTime.**

Ryker's tired but beautiful face popped into view on the screen. He was lying on his bed. The bed they had ruined together all night long. Touching, tasting, so much pleasure.

"What are you thinking?" Ryker asked, his voice gravelly and low.

"Honestly? I'm thinking about every single dirty thing we did in your bed. And your face when you came apart the last time. Jesus, Ry." Wes sighed. "We were supposed to get it all out of our system. Instead, I feel like I just got a small taste and I'm starving for more." Wes reached down with one hand to rub himself, needing some friction to ease the pain of his hard cock.

"Are you touching yourself?" Ryker asked, his sheets rustling in the background. Wes remembered the smell of those sheets the morning he left—spicy and earthy, a perfect combination of the two of them that had driven Wes out of his mind.

"Yes. I can't help it. My cock only seems to respond to one stimulus lately, and that's you," Wes said, watching Ryker's face for his reaction. Fuck holding back. It was the truth. He wanted Ryker. Again. Only. Whatever this feeling between them was, it hadn't burned itself out. Not yet.

Wes shoved his hand down his pants and swiped the pre-cum over the tip of his erection.

"I'm glad you're having the same problem," Ryker said. "But I saw the pictures from your event in Atlanta, dancing and having dinner with several hot guys. You're not short on company."

"You mean Ashton and Chase? Hah!" Wes barked out a laugh. "They're hot for each other, not me." Wes's face grew serious again. "And it was just a dance, nothing more. You're the only one I fucking want."

"Good. I feel the same way." Ryker's face flushed at his admission.

"What about Javier?" Wes asked.

Ryker's intense blue eyes stared back at him. "No. I told you I wasn't interested in him." He paused. "It's you I think about. One night together wasn't nearly enough. And just so you know, the next time you're in my bed, I'm going to slide my aching cock in your tight ass and make you mine. I'm going to fuck the cum out of you until you scream my name."

Wes's body jolted at that mental image. "Fuck, Ry, you have a dirty mouth."

"You're welcome. I can say it again in Spanish if you'd like," Ryker replied.

"*Por favor*," Wes laughed. Having a lover he could lust after and laugh with was rare. He stared at Ryker's beautiful eyes, unable to look away.

"I want you to taste yourself," Wes ordered Ryker.

"Mmm, the bossy Dom is back."

"What?"

"You're bossy in bed. I love it, turns me on." Ryker smiled slowly. "But only in bed."

Wes watched as Ryker lifted his thumb very slowly to his mouth. Ryker stuck out his talented tongue and licked his finger, then slid his tongue up and over his full lips, making them slick.

"Fuck, that's hot. How do you taste?" Wes asked, licking his own lips in response.

"Salty, musky. But not as good as you," Ryker murmured, his voice deepening.

"Show me your cock," Wes demanded.

Ryker complied. His long, hard cock came into view, dark and pulsing with need. For Wes. Only Wes.

"Imagine I'm there with you. Feel my hot breath on your dick." Wes grabbed the lube on the nightstand and quickly poured some out, giving his cock a tight, smooth slide.

"Yes, I can feel it," Ryker murmured.

"I'm sinking my hot, wet mouth over your cock, sucking it all the way down. Feel the muscles in my throat swallowing you, sucking so hard." Wes moved his hand faster and faster, watching Ryker's hand moving in tandem.

"Fuck, Wes, so close," Ryker panted.

"That's it, baby. I'm moving lower now, licking your balls, your hole, rimming you so good. Feel my hot, wet tongue in your ass."

"Wes!"

Wes watched as Ryker came apart, moaning his name as jet after jet of cum covered his cock and balls. The sight and sounds were so sexy that Wes only had to give himself one last tug before he lost it.

"Ryker!" Wes's orgasm barreled through him, hot cum covering his hand and stomach. His whole body tensed and arched, and he writhed on the bed, the euphoric tide draining his body. It was several more minutes before Wes had the lung capacity to speak again.

"I think I'm addicted to phone sex now." Wes laughed.

Ryker grinned. "I'm glad I can corrupt you so easily, Mr. Stewart."

Wes shook his head. "Okay, that shouldn't turn me on, but it does."

"I look forward to our next encounter then. *Sir.*"

"Stop. No more sexy games. I shouldn't be able to get it up that quickly again." Wes laughed, his cock twitching with renewed interest. He slowly massaged his chest, tiny shudders rippling through his body. "Are you trying to do me in?"

Ryker chuckled, his blue eyes filled with mischief. "Not until our first book is written."

"Hold on," Wes said as he removed his shirt, briefs, and pants and got under the covers. "Are you okay? Do you want to talk for a while?"

"You know, despite your ego, you're a rather sensitive man."

Wes smirked and gave his trademark wink. "Don't tell anyone."

****

Ryker

Wes and Ryker talked until two thirty in the morning, both of them sated and sleepy, but unwilling to break their connection.

The echo of Wes's voice once again lulled Ryker's mind into a deep sleep, and he woke seven hours later, refreshed and full of creative energy. And filled with strange, exhilarating feelings that made his chest ache, but in a good way. Ryker's whole body buzzed with the anticipation of seeing Wes again, touching him, hearing his voice, and looking into those warm, golden eyes.

What the fuck is going on with me? I must be watching too many rom-coms.

Ryker reasoned it was elation after finally sleeping for more than three hours. But that would be a lie.

It felt like … something more than like. He found himself thinking about Wes all the time, and the need to be with him got stronger every day. He was more than a hook-up, more than a friend and more than a writing partner. Oh, God, he felt amazing and yet terrified at the same time. This wasn't supposed to happen. He didn't catch feelings with other lovers. Was he the only one reacting this way, or did Wes feel it, too? If it was only him, he was fucked for sure. No way did he want to fall hard for Wes only to have him turn and walk away. What the fuck was he going to do?

He needed to talk to someone who had experience with relationships, and he didn't hesitate to pick up his phone.

"*Hola, mi querido.* How are you today, my son?" his mom said when she answered.

"I'm okay, Mama. I have a question, and feel free to tell me if you don't want to talk about it, but I need some advice."

"Ryker," Tina interrupted. "What is it?"

Ryker paused to clear his throat. "What happened

when you met my father? I mean, you got married very quickly. Did you fall in love that fast?"

Ryker heard his mom's indrawn breath. "Yes, it was, as the expression goes, love at first sight. Everything just clicked. Our eyes met and I knew. I knew I had to be with him. When we touched, it was so powerful that I was helpless to resist. And when we talked—him with his basic Spanish and me with very little English—well, the language barrier didn't matter. We just wanted to be with each other all the time." She sighed, sniffling. "Why do you ask this, *querido*? Is it Wes?"

He wouldn't bother to lie at this point. "I've never felt this way about a man before. Which is crazy, because at first I didn't like him—or I didn't want to like him—and now we can't stay away from each other. And I don't want anyone else. But I'm also scared shitless. Neither of us are interested in a relationship. I think." Ryker sighed and ran a hand down his chest, over his heart. "I don't know what to do. All I know is I'm a confirmed bachelor, prone to anxiety and grumpiness, who prefers to live alone. I'm set in my ways. Wes lives his life in the public eye and can have any man he wants. And now we're working together on this book."

"*Querido*, slow down. Never before have I heard you talk this way. First, you are amazing just as you are. None of us are without faults, Wes included. And sometimes differences in people balance each other out. But more importantly, this feeling you have sounds like something special. A love like that is when you feel so alive. And as it relates to your work, this is a risk, for sure. But if I didn't take a risk with your father, I wouldn't have you and Rachel, *sí*?"

"Yes, Mama, I get it. Thanks, I have a lot to think about. Well, I better go."

"I'm not done yet," she murmured. "Please call

your sister. I worry, with her working so far away in Australia. Oh, and come for dinner next Sunday. I'm making *ropa vieja* with plantains." Ryker heard her doorbell ring. "I have to go. Tell Wes I said hi. He'd better treat you right, or I will find him and he will get the wooden spoon."

Ouch, an angry mom with a weapon was something Ryker would wish upon no man.

Okay—call Rachel.

Say hi to Wes. *Wes.*

Work. Try not to think about Wes for five minutes. If possible.

Good luck with that.

Chapter Eighteen
Wes

Wes strolled along a deserted section of Baker Beach, on the outskirts of San Francisco. The cool, salty air, vivid sunshine, and blue sky combined to create a bright, beautiful mirror of his mood. Despite the jet lag, he was energized—and shocked to admit to himself the reason why.

Ryker.

Although they had only recently met, lived in two different countries, and were opposites in many ways, Wes felt a bond with Ryker, a protective and possessive feeling that he'd never experienced with any man before. It made Wes smile for no reason, and it frightened him for so many more. As both feelings warred inside of him, Wes vowed to use this newfound energy to fuel the last part of his tour and start writing again. He needed to focus less on Ryker the man and more on Ryker the writing partner. Work should come first and foremost. The rest would work itself out over time.

Wes headed back to his hotel to do just that. Three hours and one chapter later, he was perusing social media when an e-mail notification popped up.

From: Kieran Moore
Subject: Hi

Wes,

I know it's been a long time, but I wanted to reach out. I've seen you in the news recently and I can't stop thinking about you. I see from your social media posts that you'll be in Portland on the 26th. Let's meet up for coffee. My new number is attached, please call or text anytime.

Yours,

Kieran

The nerve of of his manipulative asshole ex! After all his lies, he expected Wes to forgive him and agree to reunite all these years later, like nothing happened?

Wes hit delete, blocked the e-mail, and sent a note to Luca and Grey to warn them. Then he went on with his morning.

By noon, Wes was off to another event, where he and three other best-selling authors took part in an international conference on top writing trends and topics. The quality of panelists was high, but Wes found Ethan Blackwell, a former FBI agent turned crime fiction author, the most stimulating. Ethan was a forty-year-old man with salt-and-pepper hair who looked more like a model than a former cop. He had brains, looks, and talent, and his charismatic presence had drawn huge crowds to the session. The audience lapped up his funny quips and dramatic stories.

Once the individual presentations were over, all the panelists gathered on the stage to participate in the lively Q&A portion of the event. The moderator stood up and started fielding questions.

"My question is for Ethan Blackwell," a young woman in the front row said. "How did you make the transition from active investigator to author? Was it difficult? Do you miss the thrill of hunting down leads and solving cases?"

Ethan gave a huge smile. "Good question. Actually, I still solve the case, except now I also create the crime." The audience laughed. "Truthfully, my work at the bureau was rewarding, but it was also personally draining after so many years of long hours and stressful situations. And the transition to full-time writing was pretty smooth. I still have to do a lot of research, so there's a good deal of overlap with my last job. I love what I do now, and I have no regrets."

"Next question. The woman in yellow, please." The moderator motioned to the front of the room.

A young woman with blonde hair stood up. "My question is for Wes Stewart. What are your top tips for first-time authors when it comes to writing a mystery? Oh, and are you single?" She waved coyly.

Wes faced the audience. "For question number one, focus on creating fulsome characters, and make sure to use misdirection to keep your audience engaged." He paused. "As for question two, yes, I'm single and happy. I'm way too high maintenance for most men," he joked as the audience laughed.

"Next, the man with glasses at the front," the moderator said, pointing to an older man in a suit.

"My question is for Ethan. Are all your stories based on true crimes? And have you ever been asked to go back to work, to solve cold cases, for example?" the man asked, then sat back down amongst the crowd.

"To an extent, many of my stories are inspired by crime scenes I worked on or heard about through my network. But I have no desire to go back to my former life. I'm old now, in case you haven't noticed." Ethan indicated his grey hair as the audience quietly laughed along with him. "And I have not been asked to review any cold cases." He paused. "But I wouldn't necessarily say no if I was asked. In a private capacity, of course."

Excited murmurs echoed in the conference room.

"Okay, folks, final question. The lady in red, please." The moderator pointed at a beautiful woman in a sharp red suit.

"Wes, you've been asked by several reporters in recent weeks if you're working with another author on a new series. Is that true? And if so, are you working with the man sitting beside you?" she asked, pointing to Ethan.

The crowd erupted in murmurs and squeals until the moderator broke in. "Quiet, please, so our guest can answer."

Wes looked at Ethan, but Ethan shrugged and waved at him to go. "I may or may not be working with another author on a new series. Like I've said before, you'll have to follow my social media accounts for official announcements to find out. But I can tell you that I have no current plans to work with Ethan Blackwell. Though that's not a bad idea. Ethan, what do you say?" Wes smiled and looked over at Ethan as the crowd clapped enthusiastically.

The moderator signaled to the panel that they were done, and the host concluded the event. After the crowds trickled out of the room and the mics were removed, Wes walked over to Ethan.

"Ethan, I loved your talk. I learned a lot. Would you have time for a quick drink?" he asked.

"Sounds great. How about Angler's Cove? It's a short walk from here," Ethan replied.

They left the conference venue and walked down to the waterfront, Ethan sharing his knowledge about San Francisco and his favorite places to eat and drink. They finally entered the nautical-themed bar and settled into a booth near the front of the room with a view of the water, Wes with his vodka on ice and Ethan with rye and ginger.

"So, how do you like San Francisco so far?" Ethan asked.

"I've been here before, but it gets better every time. The food, the art, the energy. It's a great city. I just wish I had more time to actually explore and see the sights when I travel." He paused. "But to be honest, my favorite city in the US is New York."

"And why's that?" Ethan asked, signaling the waiter for another round.

Because Ryker's there, was Wes's first thought, but he pushed that sentimental notion aside. "The people, the attitude, the grit. It's messy, beautiful, heartbreaking, and exhilarating all at once," Wes said.

"Sounds more like a relationship than a city," Ethan observed, cocking his head.

Wes ignored the comment and pivoted the conversation. "Tell me more about this exciting FBI life of yours."

"It wasn't all that. I mean, it was interesting for sure. I met good people and worked complex cases. It was fulfilling for a while, but then it ended up taking a huge toll on me personally. Like I said today, working long, erratic hours and dealing with shocking crime scenes takes its toll. I had issues sleeping, concentrating, and I was never home. Eventually, my wife divorced me, and I had to start over again."

"And now that you're a full-time author, things are balanced?" Wes asked.

Ethan nodded and smiled, his dark brown eyes warm. "Exactly. I have time to have a life, travel, volunteer, date. Although dating in this city is fucking murder. Sorry, man, that's a bad pun." Ethan took a long sip of his drink. "Dating is painful. There are a lot of predatory people out there. So many women are only interested in my celebrity status. I've just about given up on a romantic relationship." He sighed.

"I know what you mean about that. It's not easy. I prefer to keep things casual. I don't do relationships," Wes said. Ryker's face popped up in his mind, and he inwardly cringed at his comment. "But that's me. I'm sure there's a wonderful woman out there for you, just waiting." He clinked Ethan's glass with his own.

"Don't give up on love either. There may be a man out there who changes your life for the better.

Casual dating is okay, but to me, not nearly as satisfying as having a true partner. There's something to be said about having someone to come home to, to share life's ups and downs with, to champion each other. Someone to talk to when you wake up in the middle of the night."

The middle of the night. That mention only reminded Wes of Ryker and his nightmares. He wished he'd been there to comfort him when he woke, to hold him and assure him everything would be okay. What would that be like? To be the one Ryker woke up next to every day? Oddly enough, Wes could picture it clearly even though a small part of him was still a little bit freaked out. It was crazy how much depth of feeling he had for this man he'd only known for such a short time.

"You look deep in thought. Did I hit a nerve? If so, I apologize. I tend to run my mouth about things."

"No, it's fine. I'm just taking in everything you said. You may be right. Thank you," Wes said as he took another sip of his drink.

"So, what's the real scoop?" Ethan asked. "Are you working with another author on a new series? Don't worry, my lips are zipped."

Wes nodded. "We'll announce it formally in a couple of months. The prospect of working with a creative partner is very exciting. It's a new venture for both of us. He's a very talented author. His storytelling is so vivid, so imaginative." Wes could feel heat rising in his cheeks. *Dammit, I never blush.* "Sorry, didn't mean to get carried away there. I feel this partnership might give my writing new inspiration. The passion that's been missing for a while." He sipped his drink, lowering his eyes.

"That's good. He sounds like an amazing partner. I wish you all the best on your new collaboration." Ethan smiled knowingly as Wes's face continued to burn.

Ethan's phone vibrated suddenly. "Excuse me for a moment."

Wes sat there pondering their conversation while Ethan checked his phone and typed away.

"This was really nice, Wes, but I gotta get back to work. My agent is after me about another public appearance opportunity, and I've got a forty-eight hour deadline for my next draft."

Ethan made to pull out his wallet, but Wes intervened. "Nope, I've got it. My pleasure."

"Thanks, Wes. Hey, here are my contact details." Ethan handed over a plain black business card. "Stay in touch, okay? Who knows, maybe we can work together on a book in the future."

Wes shook Ethan's hand. "I'd like that. Take care."

Wes ordered another drink and sat quietly looking out over the harbor, taking in the sunset and enjoying the happy, frenetic atmosphere of the bar. He wondered what Ryker would think of this place, this view. He'd probably grumble about too many tourists. Then they'd sit closely together, and talk about anything and everything, and sip wine and stare at each other like no one else existed. *Jesus, I guess I'm ready to write those love scenes now.* Maybe Ethan was right. Wes's previous experience at a relationship soured him for years, but it was based on lies. Was he ready to try again? Maybe there was something to the idea of having a partner, someone to hold hands with while watching the sunset.

Half an hour later, Wes was walking back to his hotel when his phone rang. The call display said *Unknown Number.*

Wes answered. "Hello?"

"Hello, Wesley," a smooth voice murmured. "It's been a long time."

Kieran. *Fuck my life.*

"Did you get my e-mail, Wesley? I've been trying to reach you for ages, but your annoying little assistant keeps blocking my attempts," Kieran complained.

"If you're referring to Luca, he is anything but annoying or little. And why the fuck are you calling me now after three years? What do you want?" Wes demanded.

Kieran sighed. "I just want to see how you're doing, my love. I've missed you terribly. And I see from the news that you've been busy fucking everything that moves, but there's no evidence of any relationships. I guess you've never gotten over me, have you?"

Kieran's smugness ratcheted Wes's temper up ten notches. "There was nothing to get over. We had fun, you lied and betrayed me, I kicked you out on your sorry ass, end of story," Wes barked. "And there's no fucking sequel or part two. But let me guess, you're flat broke again and need money, right?" Wes heard Kieran's faint gasp on the other end of the line. "Well, tough shit. Now, I don't know how you got hold of this number, but you'd better erase it from your phone and never, ever contact me again. Got it?"

"This isn't over, Wesley. See you around," Kieran replied with a monotone voice, then hung up.

Wes dialed Luca but got his voicemail. "Hey, it's me. Kieran just called my cell. I don't know how the fuck he got my number, and his showed up as unknown, so I can't block it. Let me know if he's contacted you or Grey. Oh, and I need to make a change in my itinerary, so call me back ASAP. Thanks."

Then he texted Ryker.

Wes: **How are you? Long time no text.**

Ryker: **Busy. Sent you back your chapter with notes. I've also added another chapter for you to** review. It's very good. I think we have something here. Being on the road must be good for your writing. Your block is ebbing away.

Wes: **Not how's work. How are you?**

Ryker: **I'm okay. Still tired. Work and fur babies keeping me busy. Oh, and I have to call my sister in Australia. I need to set aside at least two hours for that.**

Wes: **She likes to talk?**

Ryker: **She's a linguistics professor so the answer is yes.**

Wes: **Interesting. Speaking of talking, I chatted with a former FBI investigator today. Very cool guy.**

Ryker: **Ethan Blackwell? Saw him on the list for your event, lucky you.**

Wes: **He's awesome but sadly into women. Besides, he isn't a grumpy New Yorker.**

Ryker: **Are you saying you like me?**

Wes paused, his earlier promise to himself to focus on their writing partnership slowly dissolving. Instead, he blurted out exactly how he felt.

Wes: **Yes. I admit it. I can't stop thinking about you.**

Ryker: **I know the feeling. Is it okay to say I miss you?**

Wes was lightheaded. Was this really happening? Was he going to reach for something more?

Wes: **I miss you too.**

Ryker: **We're sappy. Jesus, don't show anyone these texts!**

Wes: **No way. Sappy is our secret.**

Ryker: **I gotta go. Spock and Isaac are hissing and growling at each other and WW3 is about to erupt in my living room.**

Wes: **Give them all a scratch for me. Oh, and**

BTW, my writing is better now because I have a stimulating partner to work with □

Ryker: **So that means I can take all the credit when our book is a success? Cool.**

Wes: **Haha.**

Ryker: **Talk soon, safe travels.**

Wes: **C u soon.**

Luca called back and Wes had him rearrange his travel. Fuck it. He had two days before he was due to arrive in Portland, and in the meantime, there was only one place he wanted to be.

Chapter Nineteen
Ryker

4:30 PM Eastern time meant it was 6:30 AM in Sydney, Australia. Ryker got his tablet set up for a video call with his sister, Rachel, a good distraction for his consuming thoughts of Wes and how much he missed him. *Who am I right now?* He focused his attention on the task at hand and waited for his sister to dial in.

"Ryker, you shit, you haven't called me in a month! What's with that, bro?" His sister's laughing face appeared on his screen. Despite their differences in age and personality, they shared the same blue eyes and dark hair. She looked healthy, glowing. Her usual happy self.

Ryker shrugged. "Sorry, I get so caught up in my writing sometimes that I lose track of time. You know me." He smiled. "So, what's up with you, Rach? How's the weather down under?"

"Hot and sunny, honey. I'm busy as usual, but classes finish in two weeks, then finals, then grading papers, ugh. Then I'm headed back to New York, baby!" She squealed and punched a fist in the air.

Ryker laughed at his sister's antics. "Awesome. Do you know where you want to stay yet?"

"I'll bunk in with Mom."

"Okay. You're always welcome here, too," he replied.

"I know. Maybe I'll spend a week with you, split the time. As long as that's okay and I'm not crimping your style," she joked. "Oh, and I have some other good news. I was offered a tenured position at Stanford, so I'll be moving back to the US in August!" she yelled.

"Stanford! Holy shit, Rach, I'm so proud of you. Congrats! Wait, that's in San Francisco, right?"

"Close by, yup."

"I've got a friend traveling through San Francisco now on a book tour. He says the food and people are amazing." Ryker flushed just thinking about Wes.

"And who might that friend be?" she asked teasingly.

Ryker cleared his throat. "Wes Stewart. You may have heard of him."

Rachel interrupted. "The mystery author? That's fucking awesome. And he writes all those other books for wannabe authors. He's a great writer. And he's hot. And gay. So, is he a work-only friend or a friend with benefits?" she asked with a smirk.

"No comment. Next subject, please," Ryker replied, his flushed cheeks giving him away.

"Come on, Ry, spill," she cajoled.

"Nope. All I'll say, in confidence, is that he and I are working on a new book series together. We've started on some ideas. So far, so good. He's smart, charming— he knows he's charming—and despite an initial rocky start, things are moving in the right direction. And, yes, before you ask, he's even better looking in person. Next topic. How's your dating life? Any cute Aussie men catch your eye?"

"Please, with this teaching schedule and my research, who has time? Maybe when I land back in the US. Oh, wait, I know absolutely no one in California, so that means I'll probably have to use one of those dating apps. Agh!" She rolled her eyes dramatically. "I'm thirty-eight years old, Ry. I just want to find one nice, decent, extremely hot guy to settle down with. Is that too much to ask?"

"He's out there, Rach. But just to be sure, you better get your dating profile updated for your move back to the US."

"Yeah, yeah. There was something else I wanted to talk to you about, but I want you to listen to what I have to say before you respond, okay? Please don't freak out or anything." She paused and ran her hands through her hair. "I'm going to submit my DNA to one of those genealogy sites."

Ryker was stunned into silence. "Why would you want to do that?" he finally asked.

"I think it might be helpful to find out what happened to Dad," she replied quietly.

Ryker was both horrified and frightened at the turn of their conversation "Rach, he left us. Left a note saying he couldn't do it anymore and then disappeared. Never paid child support, nothing. And you want to see if we can track him down? After all these years? For what?"

"For closure. You may not need it, but I do. I need to know why the man who was so caring and loving with me just up and left. I have questions that I need answers to," she said passionately.

"You do what you feel is right, but I'm not comfortable with this. Have you told Mama? I don't want to think about him. He's not worth my time," Ryker spat out, the anger at his father simmering inside him like red-hot embers, burning slowly but never quite fading.

Her blue eyes filled with tears. "I've got to talk to her before I proceed, but I've already made up my mind. I just wanted to tell you so you were prepared," she murmured as she wiped her face.

Ryker rubbed his bracelets. "I'm sorry, but I don't know what to say about this. I think you're opening a door that is better left closed. I love you and I don't want to see you get hurt, Rach," he said, kissing his fingertips and pressing his palm to the screen. Rachel did the same, so that their hands were aligned. Just like they used to do when they were kids.

"Thanks, Ry. I love you, too. I'll be okay, I promise." She sighed and cleared her throat, back to her usual perky self. "I have a class to prepare for, so I'd better say goodbye. I'll e-mail you the details of my trip home and my moving plans once it's all arranged, okay?"

"Okay. Will you be here June fifteenth? I'm attending the Heart2Home shelter benefit and would love for you to come with."

"Definitely. Hugs and kisses to Spock, Isaac, and Princess Leia. Bye!" She waved and logged off.

Ryker stared at his laptop screen, trying to process Rachel's bombshell news about searching for their father. At thirty-three, Ryker had made peace with not knowing where his father was. But his sister obviously did not feel the same. She was older. She remembered him, and it was clear she had questions that needed answers.

Ryker's gut told him that Rachel's search might lead to difficult truths. More changes to his life were coming, and he'd better be prepared.

He needed to talk to someone. Without thinking, he dialed Wes's number.

****

Wes

So much for business before pleasure, Wes thought as he made his way past the baggage area at La Guardia Airport, hurrying to get out of the terminal. The impulse to see Ryker again was too strong for Wes to ignore, even if it meant rescheduling two days, taking a five-and-a-half-hour flight from LA to New York, going through security screening, and enduring additional transit time. By coincidence, on his flight over, Ryker had called and left a voicemail. Once Wes landed, he'd texted to let him know he was in a business meeting but would contact him as soon as possible. Something in Ryker's voice was off and it worried Wes. Maybe he wasn't sleeping again.

Wes knew as soon as he'd booked this surprise trip that he was done pretending Ryker was a casual fuck buddy. The intimate connection they shared overpowered any concern Wes had about their personal and work lives weaving toward a potentially disastrous end. Ryker's emotional grip on him was an unexpected revelation. He just hoped his surprise visit would be welcomed by Ryker's open arms.

Wes located his car service and hopped in, and another thirty minutes later he crossed the Queensboro Bridge into Manhattan. Wes's body felt more on edge now that the reunion he craved was so close at hand. He replied to several e-mails, calls, and texts to keep himself from jumping out of his skin. They pulled up to the hotel and Wes leapt out of the car, heading for the front desk to check in.

It had been a long-ass day, so Wes grabbed a quick nap and shower to recharge and a nip of bourbon to calm his nerves. Two hours later, dressed in his favorite black jeans, grey Henley, and Chelsea boots, Wes was ready to go. Grabbing his Burberry trench, he checked his phone again: 9:05 PM. He noted several texts from Luca and replied to them on the ride over. He was pacing in the lobby of Ryker's building fifteen minutes later.

As he stood there, now mere minutes away from Ryker, he replayed their last encounter in his mind. He recalled every touch and taste, and the gorgeous smile on Ryker's stunning face, his smooth, resonant voice moaning in pleasure. Their pleasure. Wes wanted more and more memories of them together, and he wondered how many times would be enough. He didn't have an answer—and he was so far gone at this point, he didn't care. Maybe it would never be enough. He was ready, and there was no turning back.

Wes: **Hey, Sleeping Beauty, you awake?**

Ryker: **Yup, watching a movie with my furry sidekicks.**

Wes: **Feel like company?**

Ryker: **FaceTime?**

Wes: **Better.**

Ryker: **???**

Wes: **I'm downstairs. Call security so I can access the elevator.**

The security guard's phone rang two seconds later, and the older man motioned Wes over.

As he stood up, a huge, fluttering sensation took flight in Wes's gut, and his whole body trembled with excitement, his hand shaking slightly as he signed in. The elevator ride felt like thirty minutes instead of thirty seconds, and as he exited, Wes's entire body clenched at the sight of Ryker leaning against the doorjamb at the end of the hallway.

Ryker was barefoot, wearing a pair of ripped, threadbare jeans, his dark hair spilling over sleek shoulders, his smooth chest and biceps on display, the veins in his arms bulging as one hand rested on his hipbone and the other high up on the door. So much hot, supple skin just waiting to be touched and explored. Wes had never seen a sexier vision in all his life than Ryker, and his dick swelled so fast and so hard he caught his breath.

Then Ryker slowly smiled, and Christ, his face transformed—it was even more stunning than Wes remembered. He wanted to be the reason that smile appeared over and over and over again. Wes's heart raced wildly at the sight of his beautiful man. Yes, that was how he thought of Ryker in this moment. His.

Wes's steps quickened. Drawing closer, he threw

his coat on the floor just outside the door and reached for Ryker's face with both hands, rubbing his stubbled cheeks with his thumbs and taking in the sight of the deep blue eyes that haunted his days and nights.

"Missed you," Ryker whispered just before their lips met.

The claiming kiss that followed echoed the sentiment.

Chapter Twenty
Ryker

Wes was here. In New York. It was not a dream, but a perfect surprise. His unanticipated arrival filled Ryker with a heady mix of shock, arousal, and pure elation.

"I missed you, too. So much," Wes whispered in between kisses as his hands moved down to grip Ryker's waist. Ryker did the same and pulled Wes in tight, savoring the excitement of their unexpected reunion. For a short while they stood in each other's arms, breathing each other's air, just taking the moment in. Ryker's gut clenched with the realization that something beyond their physical chemistry was at play. Somehow Wes belonged here, with him, and Ryker was more than happy to welcome him home.

He wondered how long Wes could stay and how many times they could make love. Ryker had never understood that term until now. But with Wes, that was exactly what it was. Their passion was far deeper and more meaningful than any sex Ryker had ever experienced.

He crushed Wes's soft mouth, his tongue plunging into that hot, sweet essence, savoring the taste of whiskey and mint. Ryker's hands moved down Wes's lower back to cup his taut ass, rubbing and squeezing those firm muscles as he pulled their hips into close contact. He punched his hips forward and rubbed their hard, aching dicks together, not caring if anyone walked into the hallway to witness their make-out session. They moaned in unison and finally came up for air, staring into each other's eyes. Ryker trailed his right hand over Wes's jaw and gently touched his heart-shaped lips, tracing them, trying to imprint their texture and softness on his memory. Then Wes playfully nipped Ryker's finger and the tender moment was gone, replaced with a powerful need to be as close as possible, skin to skin.

They needed to get naked. Right fucking now. Ryker pulled back and drew Wes inside the apartment.

"As much as I'd love to fuck you against the wall in the hallway, I think my neighbors might complain," he said wryly, reaching for Wes again.

"Mmm, I don't think so. They'd be lucky to witness such a sexy sight," Wes said as they continued to kiss and grope each other.

"You're supposed to be headed to LA," Ryker managed to say between fervent kisses.

Wes slid a hand around the nape of Ryker's neck and brought their foreheads together, looking deep into his eyes. Ryker took a deep breath to let this perfect moment sink in.

"I had to see you. I couldn't wait another week, two weeks. I know this is crazy, but I need you," Wes whispered, taking Ryker's mouth again in a kiss so scorching hot, Ryker thought he might melt on the spot.

"I know the feeling. You've got way too many clothes on." Ryker tugged on Wes's Henley, pulling it up over his head and tossing it aside. He took a moment to appreciate the sight of Wes's golden pecs and defined abs before yanking on the buttons of his jeans, eager to uncover that big, pulsing cock.

Wes stepped out of his jeans and briefs and kicked them away. He leaned against the wall, grabbing his dick in one hand and tugging, his rock-hard erection leaking pre-cum. Ryker's mouth watered at the sight of his man, one stray lock of blond hair hanging over his forehead, tiny beads of sweat rolling down his neck, those glowing hazel eyes locked onto him. Wes licked his lips and smiled, offering a grin so full of sinful mischief that Ryker answered with a smile of his own.

"Take off your jeans," Wes said as he continued to stroke himself.

Ryker slowly opened his button fly, taking his time, teasing, amping up their mutual desire. But before he could get to the third button, Wes reached out and yanked Ryker's jeans open and shoved them down. He stepped out of his pants, and suddenly Wes lifted Ryker into his arms. Ryker's back hit the wall and he gasped in shock, both amazed and turned on at Wes's strength, loving the feel of all that warm, naked skin rubbing against his own.

"No more teasing, baby. I'm too far gone," Wes murmured, taking Ryker's mouth again, nibbling and licking. "Bed. Now," he said in that deep, commanding voice. "I need you to fuck me."

With that demand, Ryker's whole body shivered. Ryker locked his legs around Wes's waist as Wes carried him to the bedroom, and they tumbled together onto the covers. He scrambled to reach the lube and condoms from his bedside drawer and threw them on the bed as Wes licked his way down his stomach. Ryker gasped and lay back, spread-eagle.

"Do we need condoms?" Wes asked, running his big, warm hands up Ryker's thighs and over to his cock, the touch setting off flickers of excitement with every movement. "There's no one else. We've both been tested recently, and I only want you."

Ryker's entire body jolted at the thought, and he nodded. "No condoms." He sighed, rubbing Wes's biceps. "I can't wait to watch my cum dripping out of your perfect ass."

Wes grabbed his own dick. "God, I love your filthy mouth," he moaned.

Ryker smiled, poured the lube in his hands, and started to stroke his dick. "Lie back," he ordered.

They switched places. Wes spread himself out on the bed, all six feet of his stunning male form on display, muscles straining, his uncut cock rigid and begging for relief.

Ryker pushed Wes's legs apart, then bent forward and swallowed Wes's dick down his throat in one long, smooth move, sucking hard and humming to increase Wes's pleasure. "Ryker, so deep," Wes moaned, moving his head from side to side, as if he couldn't bear the sensation. Ryker eased off Wes's dick with a wet *pop* and moved lower to his heavy balls, inhaling deeply, nuzzling his nose into Wes's musky scent and suckling first one, then the other. Ryker pushed Wes's knees back to his chest, exposing his hole.

"Ryker, please," Wes panted, and Ryker obeyed, licking Wes's taint and then his puckered rim, pushing his tongue past the tight muscle, easing the constriction, teasing the nerve endings.

Wes pushed his ass closer, moaning and writhing. "Yes, more."

Ryker continued to tongue Wes's tight hole while stroking himself, making sure that Wes was nice and relaxed, edging him until he noticed Wes's balls tighten.

"Fuck me," Wes growled. "Hurry!"

Ryker reared up, slathering lube on his cock. Then he got on his knees between Wes's legs and pushed his slick prick into Wes's hole, watching as his long cock was swallowed up by Wes's tight heat. The lack of condom made every sensation hotter, sharper. Ryker trembled all over with the pure bliss of the moment.

"So hot. I can feel all of you," Ryker whispered in amazement. "It's so fucking good."

He moaned, pushing his hips forward. Once fully

seated, he grabbed Wes's dick and started pumping it in time with his thrusts. Ryker's balls slapped Wes's ass as he pounded out a rough rhythm, and the dirty sound reverberated in the bedroom, accompanying their moans of pleasure. Ryker's senses were suddenly overwhelmed by every single aspect of their lovemaking, and he looked down into Wes's eyes, tears welling up. *This man is going to ruin me*, Ryker thought as he continued to piston his hips frantically, shifting slightly to find the angle that would hit Wes's prostate.

"Don't stop!" Wes pleaded, his voice hoarse from crying out. "Right there!"

"So close, *mi amor*," Ryker whispered as he continued thrusting, and suddenly he felt Wes's entire body tense, his muscles locking.

"Ry!" he yelled, and his hot cum covered Ryker's hand.

Ryker watched his beautiful man come apart, his body shaking, his face lit with pleasure. Wes licked his lips, his golden eyes capturing Ryker's, and that was it.

"*Mi corazon*," Ryker groaned, the force of his orgasm spreading to every part of his body, the feeling so intense, Ryker had salty tears trickling down his face, mixing with drops of sweat as he rode the wave of satisfaction. He continued to pump his lover full of cum, wanting to mark and claim Wes as his and only his.

"Ryker, baby, I can feel you inside me," Wes whispered frantically.

As they both floated down from their explosive climax, Ryker slowed the movement of his hips and eventually, reluctantly, withdrew from Wes's body.

"God, my cum dripping out of your sexy ass is the hottest thing I've ever seen in my life," Ryker said to Wes as he stroked Wes's hole, unable to look away from the evidence of their joining. Ryker leaned over his lover, kissing Wes deeply, their hands now roaming all over each other, slower now, savoring each touch and taste as if they were just getting started.

Ryker rolled onto his back as Wes snuggled up against him, throwing his leg over Ryker's. "Rest up, Sleeping Beauty. It's my turn next."

****

Wes

Coming here was the right decision, Wes told himself as his well-used body lay snug against Ryker's, satiated and happy. He couldn't stop rubbing and touching Ryker, his lover's lean muscles still warm and supple from their powerful lovemaking.

In one of the rare moments of his life, Wes was speechless. He'd never had sex that intense before, like he and Ryker were trying to forge not just their bodies but their souls into one being. Then he'd felt the unexpected tears on his face as he reached his climax and saw the same evidence mirrored on Ryker's face. When those blue eyes filled and turned liquid, Wes completely lost his heart to the quiet man now lying beside him.

I'm in love, he admitted to himself and couldn't quite believe it. *Shit, this is so fast and crazy, but so right.*

They'd both said they weren't looking for a relationship, but it was too late. Wes was too far gone over this man to turn back. He was going to ride this wave all the way to shore. He wasn't completely sure of Ryker's feelings, and he knew he'd have to tread very, very carefully. His man liked his routine, and this relationship was definitely outside of that.

Wes closed his eyes to rest for a few minutes. When he blinked and opened them, he realized he was alone in bed, and the room was darker. The blinds were now closed. As he got his bearings, he noticed a glass of water on the nightstand.

Wes pushed himself up and leaned against the suede headboard, taking a long sip of water to quench his thirst. He enjoyed the quietness of the room, taking in his surroundings and savoring the smell of their sex, and it was so fucking amazing that Wes's dick started to swell again. Just as he was about to get up and go looking for Ryker, his partner entered the bedroom. Wearing low-slung track pants, Ryker carried a wood tray filled with charcuterie, fruit and cheese. He placed it on the nightstand, then got back in bed, leaning over to brush a soft kiss over Wes's lips.

"Did you enjoy your nap?" Ryker asked, smiling against his mouth.

"I did. What time is it?" Wes asked.

"It's just after midnight. You zonked out cold for a good two hours, and I didn't want to wake you. Especially after all your travel to get here. So I took a shower and did some writing." Ryker grabbed the tray and placed it on the bed between them. "Then I got hungry and figured you would be, too, when you woke, so I brought snacks." He smiled as he grabbed a cracker, placed a slice of brie cheese on top, and shoved it in his mouth.

"Mmm. Mind-blowing sex and food on demand. I may never leave," Wes quipped as he munched on prosciutto.

Ryker coughed. "Sorry, crumbs," he explained as his cheeks began to flush.

"You okay there, love?" Wes asked, keeping a straight face as he tested the romantic waters.

"Yup. Wait. Love?" Ryker asked with wide eyes.

Wes laughed. "It's a British term. You know, 'how are you, love?' Why, does it bother you?" Wes asked, curiously gauging Ryker's response.

"Not at all. Big boy." Ryker chuckled.

"Big *no*," Wes replied, shaking his head.

Ryker's brows knit together. "Big dick?"

Wes grinned smugly. "That's more like it."

"No way. Your ego does not need any more inflating."

"Speaking of inflating." Wes pointed to his now very excited dick tenting the sheets.

"Mmm, big dick it is. Sweetheart," Ryker murmured, and now it was Wes's turn to blush.

Shit, why do I like that so much?

Wes made a show by attempting to throw a grape in his mouth, but he missed and it dropped to his chest instead.

"Your hand-eye coordination is way off," Ryker quipped.

"It's perfect. Watch." This time, the grape successfully landed in his mouth, and he munched away. "You just distracted me the first time." Wes grabbed another grape and some cheese. "You left a voicemail when I was on my way here. You sounded odd. What's going on?"

"I told you I needed to chat with my sister," Ryker said, and Wes nodded. "Well, the good news is, she's accepted a tenured position at Stanford and will be moving back to the US in August."

"Good for her. Sounds like an amazing opportunity. Are you happy?" Wes asked.

"Very. Even if she's on the West Coast, at least we can visit more often." He paused. "It was her other news that I'm struggling with. She wants to submit her DNA to a genealogy site to see if it might help in locating our father's whereabouts."

Wes paused to look over Ryker's face. "And

you're understandably concerned for her, and upset, and also wondering, why now?" Wes replied, as if he'd read Ryker's mind.

"Yes, exactly. I'm afraid of what might happen. What if she finds him and he's still alive? Will she want to see him, have a relationship with him? What if he still has no answers for her? Or refuses to see her? Or what if he's dead? I know she struggles with why he left, but what good will this do except resurrect all the pain?"

Wes leaned in and rubbed his thumb over Ryker's cheek. "I'm sure you struggle with his leaving, too. I know you have no recollection of him, but you see the pain in your mom and sister, and you want to take that away."

"I do. And to be honest, I like my life the way it is. I may be angry with my father, but I've made peace with how things turned out. I don't know that any good will come of digging up old history."

"Dealing with past trauma is never easy, and everyone has their own way of coping. It took me years of therapy to deal with my parents' death, and when the man responsible was brought to trial years later, unfortunately, it brought it all back up again. But I had a good support system and came out stronger. Maybe not happier, but stronger." Wes smiled wanly. "Just like you did after that man attacked you. Eventually, you found your way out."

"I guess we're not all that different," Ryker said.

"No, we're not," Wes offered with a smile, moving closer. "I understand where both you and your sister are coming from. She needs answers and is determined to get them. Part of you may also want those answers, but you don't think you're ready yet."

Ryker sighed. "I don't think I am, but I may not have a choice. I've always supported her no matter what, and this should be no different."

"You're a good man with a sensitive heart, and your sister is lucky to have you." Wes smiled as Ryker leaned in to kiss him.

Ryker eventually sat back, and they continued to snack and talk.

"Man, I am wiped from traveling, but let me tell you, I am so glad I got to visit New Orleans on this tour. Reminds me a bit of New York. It's fun and romantic and full of strange characters." Wes paused. "I was thinking maybe we could set book two there. What do you think?"

Ryker wiped crumbs off his chest and placed the empty tray on the nightstand. "Considering we've just started writing book one, I don't know. Maybe? It could be cool. Maybe we could take a weekend trip together and see if it inspires both of us." Ryker flushed. "I mean, if that's something you want to do. If you think it's a good idea. Or not. Fuck!" Ryker grabbed the sheet and pulled it over his head to hide.

Wes was totally charmed by Ryker's fluster, and he yanked the sheet back.

"Don't hide from me, hot stuff," he teased. "And, yes, a weekend trip with you is definitely a good idea." He paused. "It's not just what I want. It's what I need." Wes reached over and took Ryker's warm cheeks in his hands, giving him a sweet kiss.

Ryker rested their foreheads together. "Are you okay?" he asked quietly, rubbing his hand down Wes's thigh and over his ass.

Wes gave a big sigh and leaned in, nuzzling his nose on Ryker's stubbled cheek. "It was perfect," he said hoarsely. "My ass is sore, but that's because I haven't bottomed in quite a while. But it was… I'm a writer who can't come up with enough words for how good it was." He reached for Ryker again, kissing his swollen pout. "It was so good, love, that I want to do it again and again," he whispered as he pushed Ryker down on the bed.

Wes deftly removed Ryker's track pants and kissed his way up long calves and taut thighs that were lightly dusted with dark hair, and finally, finally over to Ryker's long cock, which was leaking and begging for attention. Wes licked the large vein on Ryker's prick, teasing just under the head, then swirling his tongue up and around.

Ryker's hands reached for Wes, tugging his hair to lift his head.

"I'm too amped up for a slow seduction. Hurry up and fuck me," Ryker panted, rolling over onto his stomach and rising up to his knees. Wes took a moment to look his fill at Ryker's firm ass, then bent over to kiss and nip each perfect cheek before moving over to his crease. Wes spread Ryker's ass cheeks and swallowed hard at the sight of his lover's tight hole. He leaned forward and licked him from taint to tailbone.

"Wes!" Ryker cried out.

Wes lubed up his fingers and pressed one, then another inside Ryker, crooking them to peg his prostate.

Ryker's body jolted. "Wes, please," he whimpered.

Wes obeyed his lover, lubing himself up. He got on his knees and lined up his cock with Ryker's hole, pushing in at a slow, steady pace, the unreal heat and tightness of Ryker's body enveloping Wes's dick so good, he never wanted to leave. Wes placed one hand on Ryker's shoulder and the other on his waist, then tilted his hips and began thrusting at a punishing tempo.

"Touch yourself," Wes demanded, and Ryker complied, using his right hand to tug his cock.

Wes slid his hand from Ryker's shoulder down the middle of his back, touching the colorful tattoos of the moon, the sun, and, finally, the blazing comet, tracing its fiery path down until he reached his ass. It was just one more beautiful part of this man he was so crazy about.

"You're mine," Wes murmured as he squeezed Ryker's ass. "Say it."

"Yes," Ryker whispered. "I'm yours, only yours."

"Mine," Wes grunted, changing the angle, his hips moving at a furious pace.

"Yes, don't stop!" Ryker moaned as he pumped himself with his hand, faster and faster, and Wes obliged. Wes needed Ryker to come first, always first. His lover's pleasure was paramount. He punched his hips forward again, and suddenly, Ryker's hole clenched tighter around Wes's cock.

"Wes!" Ryker screamed.

Wes felt his balls tighten in response, and he gave himself over to his orgasm, the overwhelming heat of Ryker's depths his undoing. "Baby!" Wes yelled out as the intense heat of his cum filled up Ryker's ass. He slowed his movements, running his hands all over Ryker's back and ass.

Ryker collapsed on the bed and Wes followed. He stretched his larger body over Ryker, their hot skin joined from head to toe. Wes put his hands over Ryker's, interlocking their fingers, then placed soft kisses on Ryker's shoulders and neck, reveling in the feeling of total bliss.

"Too heavy?" Wes asked between deep breaths.

"Just right," Ryker murmured, tightening his fingers, then slowly drawing Wes's palm to his lips and kissing it gently, sweetly. Wes's body quivered at the intimate gesture.

"Just right" summed it up perfectly. This moment, this man, and everything Wes felt when they were together was just right.

Chapter Twenty-One
Ryker

Ryker and Wes fell into a deep sleep after their second round of lovemaking. Ryker woke up shortly after seven, his body still wound tight around Wes, their legs and arms tangled together as Wes snored gently. Ryker took the opportunity to quietly study Wes's beautiful face, taking in the long lashes fanning out over freckled cheekbones, the swollen lips, the dark blond stubble. He still couldn't believe that Wes had changed his itinerary and flown out here. For him. Ryker was so affected by this man, he was at a loss for words. Ryker fell a little bit more in love every minute they spent together. Was this crazy? A bad idea, given their work partnership? Should he be worried?

Yes, yes, and yes.

But for once in his life, Ryker ignored his rational brain and let his feelings guide him.

But the sexy morning wake-up Ryker had anticipated with Wes was rudely interrupted by Spock pushing open the bedroom door, jumping on the bed, and licking their faces.

"Whoa, Spock, stop it!" Ryker couldn't help but laugh as his excited pooch jumped between him and Wes, unable to decide who he was more excited to see. Wes lifted his head, his blond hair sticking up every which way and his hazel eyes sleepy. He grinned when Spock nuzzled his face and licked his jaw.

"Oh, Spock, thank you for the morning kiss, even though I was kind of hoping your daddy would get to me first," he joked as the dog wagged his tail in Ryker's face.

"That's life with fur babies, right? We come in second." Ryker winked as he grabbed Spock and hauled him into his arms. "I put them in the spare bedroom last night, but I must've forgot to push the door fully closed. He's a bit eager for some loving."

"I can see that." Wes smirked and leaned forward, capturing Ryker's lips in a slow, sultry morning kiss, which was rudely interrupted by Spock's wet nose poking between them.

Ryker reared his head back and laughed. "Okay, sweetheart, let's go for a walk."

"Have fun, Spock," Wes murmured as he stretched out on his back.

"I was talking to you, big dick." Ryker smirked at Wes, who threw back the covers and rolled out of bed.

"Slave driver," Wes said as he sat up again and finally got out of bed. He made a big production of stretching his arms over his head, providing Ryker with a close-up view of his naked body.

Ryker's smirk faded as he zeroed in on Wes's perfect ass, marred only by Ryker's love bites. Wes turned his head and waggled his eyebrows. "Caught ya." He laughed, then sauntered into the bathroom.

Ten minutes later, Ryker and Wes walked out into the warm spring air to stroll through Central Park. Spock took the opportunity to sniff every single post, person, and tree trunk along the way. On their way back, they stopped by a French-style bakery for chocolate croissants and headed back up to the apartment. Ryker made *café con leche*, and they spread out in the living room. The two cats wandered over and immediately jumped on Wes, willfully ignoring their owner.

Ryker was afraid to ruin their limited time together with potentially awkward relationship talk, but he knew he couldn't put it off forever. He'd have to find the right time. And the right words. Ryker rubbed his bracelets absently.

"I notice you wear those bracelets all the time. Is there any special meaning to them?" Wes asked.

"No special meaning. I count the beads or rub them if I'm feeling anxious. I guess they're sort of like worry beads. And, according to Cal, they're hipster cool, so you know, I make a fashion statement," Ryker rolled his eyes.

"They suit your Zen-meets-rockstar style." Wes gently grasped Ryker's wrist to take a closer look. "I like the color and texture. It's very natural and warm, just like you."

They kissed again.

"Hey," Ryker whispered against Wes's lips, deciding that it was now or never. "So, I'd like to keep seeing you, exclusively, and not just to write our books." Ryker held his breath, his gaze roving over Wes's face, gauging his reaction.

Wes's golden eyes glowed even brighter when he smiled. "I want that, too. I think I made that clear when I suggested we forego the condoms and I agreed to go away with you for the weekend," he teased, but then shifted his tone. "It may not be easy, though, with you living here and me in Toronto, and our books, and my travel. Are you sure you want to make a go of it?"

Ryker opened his mouth to answer, but Spock's bark interrupted them. Ryker laughed and pointed to his brown-eyed pooch, who was sitting directly in front of them.

"That's a yes!"

****

Wes

I'm in a relationship. Say it again. *I'm in a relationship*.

Wes was still in shock. Wait until he told Grey. And Luca. Well, Luca already knew given Wes's change in travel plans, but he hadn't talked to him since. He had a feeling he was due for some serious razzing by his closest friends once they found out he was trying out monogamy for the first time in three years. Especially since he'd sworn he'd never put himself in that vulnerable position again. But Wes didn't give a fuck— he was so happy, he didn't care what they would say.

After their talk over breakfast, Wes and Ryker showered together and made their way back to bed for two hours, where the sex was slow and sensual. But then they had to return to reality. Wes needed to make work calls, so Ryker showed him the den and the sleek, modular desk where he could set up his laptop.

"I've got to call my agent back anyway, so I'll be a while. Take all the time you need," Ryker said.

With that, Wes settled in and used FaceTime to call Luca.

Luca's smiling face and green-tipped hair popped up on the screen. "Good afternoon, Mr. Romance," he said with a chuckle.

"Jesus, please don't call me that. Ever."

"How about *Sleepless in LA*? No, this is more like *When Harry Met Sally*. Sorry, *When Wes Met Ryker*! Was your reunion like that scene in *The Notebook?* Did you sweep Ryker up into your arms and kiss him in the rain?" Luca joked.

Wes *had* lifted Ryker up his arms in the hallway at one point and carried him to bed, but he wasn't about to give Luca any more romantic ammunition with which to tease him.

"Are you done?" Wes couldn't help but laugh at his friend's antics. "Get it out of your system, Luca. I did call about actual work, so maybe we could get to that? Have you reworked my schedule? When do I fly out to Portland?"

"Wait a minute. You—Wesley Stewart, sworn bachelor—rearranged two days in your schedule to fly back to New York to be with Ryker, and you think I'm just gonna let that go? Come on, Wes, you know me. Tell me everything! Was Ryker surprised? How much sex did you have? Are you two officially a couple?"

Wes's face heated at the mention of the word *couple*.

"I'm only going to say this once, because this conversation is really painful for me. Yes, he was very happy to see me. I will not answer the second question, but you can take a guess based on the permanent grin on my face. And finally, yes, we're a couple. And exclusive. Happy now? I haven't even told Grey yet." Wes watched the screen as Luca's face lit up.

"Oh, my God, I am so happy for you, Wesley! Wait, I only met Ryker on that video call the other day. Please tell me I can interrogate him to make sure he's good enough for you."

Wes laughed. "You have his number. Call him up if you'd like."

"Already added it to my to-do list. So, you haven't told anyone else yet?" Wes shook his head, and Luca continued, "Can I be the one to tell Big Mac? I really want to witness his head exploding from this news. Do you think he'll be okay, or will he freak out over the implications for the book deal?"

"I don't know, and I honestly don't care if Mac is pissed. This relationship was the last thing I expected, but it feels right. And I'm not changing my mind. That being said, he is Ryker's friend, so I would prefer that Ryker tells him what's going on."

"You know, New York would be a fabulous setting for a fall wedding," Luca hinted, clearly looking for any excuse to get his event planning business underway.

"Stop right there. We just agreed to see each other. Save your wedding planning for someone else."

"Speaking of planning, I re-booked your travel. You're on the eight forty-five flight tomorrow morning. Hotel and all the other deets are being sent to your inbox as we speak. Anything else I can do?"

"I'm good. Thanks, Luca. Talk to you soon."

Wes ended the call and headed to the living room in search of his partner in crime. Ryker was standing in front of his writing board, adding Post-it notes while Spock sat at his feet. Wes noticed that Ryker was wearing his black-rimmed glasses again, the ones that made him look like a sexy, albeit longer-haired, version of Clark Kent. The sudden image of Ryker naked except for his specs got Wes hot. Again. *Jesus, this man is going to be the death of me.* It was at that moment that Ryker turned and smiled knowingly at Wes.

"How's it going, Mr. Romance?" Ryker doubled over laughing.

"You heard that? I guess Luca is a bit loud. Jesus. I have to call Grey next. He's going to be just as bad."

Ryker shrugged. "Don't worry, Cal and Mac will do the same to me. We'll just annoy them all with lots and lots of PDA." He smirked.

"You're an evil genius," Wes murmured as he wrapped his arms around Ryker from behind and pulled him in tight, Wes's suddenly stiff prick finding a perfect home in the crease of Ryker's luscious ass.

"So, when do you leave?" Ryker asked, tilting his head to the side as Wes nuzzled his neck and nipped at his ear.

"I have to be at the airport by seven tomorrow morning. Which means we only have another fifteen and a half hours together. Which means we need to get naked.

Now."

"I thought you'd never ask."

Chapter Twenty-Two
Wes

Wes was the only person standing in line at airport security with an idiotic grin on his face.

Everyone else looked grumpy and tired, given the hour, but Wes was so filled up with the happy, warm feelings Ryker inspired that he was floating on a natural high. He probably looked it, too, since the large man waving him over to the X-ray machine narrowed his eyes when he drew near. Shit, the last thing he needed was a delay in transit and a full-body search.

Wes checked his phone for the thirtieth time, infatuated with the recent selfie he'd taken as a screen saver. They'd been lying in Ryker's bed shortly before Wes left, leaning against the headboard while Spock, Isaac, and Princess Leia surrounded them. Wes had said something ridiculous, and he'd managed to capture Ryker's biggest smile, the one that made very few appearances, and even then, only for the lucky few. Wes loved that smile and wanted to see it. Every. Fucking. Day. They were looking at each other, their eyes locked together in a moment of pure happiness.

Wes stared at his phone until reality intruded. "Sir, please place your bag and all electronics in the bin," the security officer said.

Complying with the order, Wes managed to get through security and into the first-class lounge in record time. While waiting to board, he figured now was as good a time as any to call Grey.

"Hey, Wes, how's it going?" Grey answered in his usual calm tone.

"I'm good. At the airport, headed to Portland. Just wanted to call and chat."

"Isn't it the middle of the night in LA?" Grey asked.

"I'm in New York, not LA." Wes took a deep breath, his body suddenly filled with nerves. "That's part of the reason I called. I wanted to tell you before you read about it on a gossip site. Ryker and I are dating. Each other. Exclusively. We're in a relationship." Wes realized he was babbling. "And that's it."

There was a momentary pause before Grey burst out laughing. "Are you serious? Aren't you the same man who once said relationships make you break out in hives?"

Grey continued to laugh as Wes rubbed his neck and rolled his eyes. "Okay, okay, so I got burned once and it soured me on anything long term. Or anything more than one night. But shit happens, things change," Wes said.

"Shit happens? Wow, don't tell Ryker that's how you described meeting him." Grey chuckled, then cleared his throat. "But seriously, I'm happy for you. I could see the chemistry between you two when we were at Mac's, but I just assumed you would stay away from each other, given the potential business relationship."

"We couldn't stay away. He's amazing. And it's not just the sex. We talk about everything. We have this insane connection. I can't explain it. But the sex is fucking unreal. I just look at him and it's all I can do not to rip his clothes off." Wes was getting hot again, and he yanked on his shirt collar. Nearby passengers gave him the side eye. *Shit, maybe lower your voice and calm down.*

Grey coughed. "TMI, Wes. Keep that to yourself. Anyway, are you set for your last stop in Portland?"

"I'm pumped up. More interviews, the last writers' conference, and I'm done. When that's over, I'm headed home for a rest, and then back to New York to see my man."

"*Your man*? Who the fuck are you?" Grey asked.

"I don't know, but I feel fucking amazing!" Wes yelled. Heads all around him turned to stare. He mouthed a quick *sorry* to the other waiting passengers.

"...bothering you, has he?"

"What? Sorry, I didn't catch that."

"Wes, I need you to concentrate for a few minutes while I'm talking. Can you do that?" Grey paused. "Has Kieran contacted you again?"

Wes's good mood suddenly shifted downward. "Not since a few days ago. Why?" he asked.

"He's been e-mailing and calling my office, saying you're getting back together. I know it's bullshit, but he's been aggressive. All this to say, watch your back. If he crosses a line, you may need to get a restraining order. It might also be a good idea to stick a PI on him to see why he's resurfaced. My guess is he needs money."

Wes scratched his head and leaned forward. "Yeah, that's my instinct, too. I'll reach out to Luca to get a PI on retainer just in case. As for the rest, I'll be aware. Thanks for looking out for me, as always."

"No problem. Look, I've got a shitload of work piling up, but we'll talk soon, okay? Safe travels."

"Thanks. See you in a week."

Wes was checking his phone again when an announcement interrupted. *"Flight number 671 to Portland is now boarding. First-class passengers are asked to please proceed to Gate 31."*

Wes sent a few more texts and boarded his flight. He was getting seated when his phone pinged and a picture of Ryker with Spock popped up.

Ryker: **We miss you already xoxo.**

Wes: **I miss you more.**

****

Ryker

Getting out of bed after a twenty-four-hour sexathon was not easy. Every muscle ached, in the best of ways, and Ryker's mind was all over the place. Wes had done something to his concentration because all Ryker could do was lie there and smile.

Reality intruded when his phone beeped with a reminder about his video call with his agent at eleven. But before that, Ryker needed to talk to Mac and Cal before his relationship became public knowledge. He decided a group text would be the most comfortable way for him to get the conversation going.

Ryker: **You guys busy?**

Cal: **Sorta.**

Mac: **Yes.**

Of course, Mac was busy. The man was an even bigger workaholic than Ryker.

Ryker: **I have news.**

Cal: **Something good I hope?**

Mac: **Please tell me it's related to the book deal!**

Ryker: **Kinda. It's personal.**

Mac: **K. What's up?**

Ryker: **Wes and I are seeing each other.**

Mac: **Group call. NOW.**

Ryker's phone lit up. He prepared himself for the barrage of questions.

"Hey, guys."

"Hey yourself. What do you mean, you're seeing each other? You're writing a new book series together, so I imagine you'll see him occasionally. Please tell me that's what you meant," Mac growled.

"No, Mac, I mean Wes and I are dating. As in we are sleeping together. In fact, he flew out two nights ago to surprise me. We like spending time together. Naked and clothed. That sort of seeing," Ryker said.

Before Mac could say anything, Cal's voice boomed out. "I knew it! I knew it. He could not resist your moody charm. I saw it on his face when you were leaving Mac's party. So, tell us—how's the sex? He's bossy in bed, isn't he?"

Mac groaned loudly and Ryker sighed.

"Just trust me when I say it's all very good."

Mac apparently wasn't done yet, though. "Have you thought this through, Ry? Are you sure you can handle working and sleeping with this guy? What happens when you break up? What about the book deal?"

"Let him enjoy himself, Mac," Cal warned.

"No, I am being the voice of reason here, because I'm the only one who's thinking with his brain and not his dick right now," Mac barked.

Ryker took a deep breath to steady himself. "Mac, I know it's fast and unexpected, but I'm happy. We're happy together. I don't know why, but we clicked and I'm going with my gut. You need to trust me on this."

"It's not you I don't trust. I just don't want to see you get hurt, Ry. I want you to think about this realistically. He lives in Toronto. You live here. You both have busy careers and schedules. How's that gonna work out?" Mac asked.

Ryker was aware of the long-distance issue, but he wasn't too concerned right now. To be honest, he was going on instinct, just as he'd told Mac.

"We'll sort that out later. For now, we're taking it day by day."

Mac grunted. "Until he grows bored, goes hunting, gets photographed with some hot guy coming out of a nightclub, and you're left shattered."

Wes's personal history via social media flashed through Ryker's mind. Wes wanted to be exclusive, but was he prepared for the reality? Would he get restless as Mac suggested? Ryker believed that Wes was true to his word. He would have to trust in that for now.

"Wes wouldn't do that. We're seeing each other exclusively. We've even ditched the condoms."

"What the fuck, Ry? Don't do that!" Mac yelled.

"I've never had sex without condoms. Does it really feel better? I need details," Cal asked.

"This is crazy," Mac said.

Ryker interrupted Mac before he could say anything further. "Relax, we've both been tested recently, and I know what I'm doing. Be my friend. Be happy for me. I don't expect you to understand, but I need to know you two have my back."

"Of course," Mac mumbled.

"Always," Cal replied.

Ryker was mentally wrung out from this conversation. He'd expected a razzing by his friends, but Mac's cynical reaction was making him second guess his decision to be with Wes. *Fuck that.* He and Wes knew what they were doing and they were happy. On to the next item.

"Okay, now that my personal life has been dissected, let's move on. The Heart2Home shelter benefit is next month, on June fifteenth. I've bought a table and was hoping you guys would join me, please and thanks."

"Of course!" Cal exclaimed.

"Sure," Mac muttered.

"Great, I'll text you the details. Anyway, I know you guys are busy, and I have to get back to work. We'll talk soon, okay?"

"Yup. If you have time, let's meet up this week,

Ry. I'll text you," Cal said.

"Later" was all Mac said before he hung up.

And with that out of the way, Ryker was able to focus on work again. The relationship between the protagonists in their book was heating up, and Ryker now had some very personal inspiration to guide him.

Chapter Twenty-Three
Wes

Several days passed in a blur. Portland was notably colder and gloomier than New York, but Wes was busy morning until night with interviews and book signings, so he had no time to be concerned about the weather.

Tonight was the final event on his tour, a formal dinner at the Kensington Event Center in honor of the Northwest Writers Guild's fiftieth anniversary. The venue was built in the lavish style of the roaring twenties and had recently been renovated with modern touches. It was fitting, then, that tonight's *Great Gatsby* theme had the guests dressed up in classic tuxedos and fringed flapper dresses.

Normally, Wes enjoyed parties of any kind, but the past few weeks on the road had started to grind. Once this was over, he would gladly shove his tux in the closet for a while. He needed to go home and see his dogs and his friends and then head back to New York. Maybe convince Ryker to hop on a plane with him to some sunny destination with a private beach and no Internet access. Preferably clothing optional. Definitely no tuxedo.

But for now, he would enjoy the evening. He adjusted his bow tie in the large antique mirror in the lobby and watched the reflection of well-dressed guests walking by behind him, holding elegant cocktails and sampling canapés.

A young man in a white tuxedo approached, gesturing to the ballroom entrance. "Mr. Stewart, so glad you could make the dinner this evening. I'm Ron Granger, the assistant coordinator for the event. You'll be seated at table two along with your guest. If you'd care to follow me, please," he said smoothly.

"Sorry, did you say guest? I'm here on my own. There's no one attending with me," Wes said, confused.

"My apologies, sir, but he did have a ticket, and he said he was your partner. He showed me a picture of the two of you, so naturally I let him in," Ron blustered, glancing at his phone while texting rapidly.

"Where is this man now?" Wes asked.

"He's already seated." Ron pointed to the table in the corner, near the front of the stage. "The man with the red bow tie."

There were reams of people walking back and forth in the ballroom, searching for their seats and chatting along the way, obstructing his view. When the crowd finally cleared, Wes looked over at the table and spotted him.

There was no mistaking who it was. The man was slender and decked out in a sharp black tuxedo, his short, dark hair slicked with pomade in the style of tonight's theme. He had wide-set eyes, an overly thin nose, and a pouty mouth. An older man approached the table, and the man with the red bow tie smiled with glowing white teeth, like a predatory barracuda ready to snatch up its next victim. That smile was calculated and designed solely for selfish purposes—to lure in wealthy men. Wes should know.

Kieran. The little shit.

Wes smiled briefly. "It's all right, Mr. Granger, I will deal with my *guest* personally."

He proceeded to make his way through the crowd toward the table. He was stopped en route by several guests demanding selfies, which he obliged. Wes made it to his table just as Kieran was getting cozy with the older gentleman sitting beside him, his long fingers rubbing the man's thigh slowly. *Some things never change.*

"Kieran, what an unwelcome surprise. What the fuck are you doing here?" Wes bellowed, unconcerned about the guests at the table or the general audience around them. Heads turned and chatter quieted as the two men faced off.

Kieran gave the same practiced smile that had once charmed him. "Wesley, babe, don't be angry. I just wanted to see you," he simpered. He stood and leaned in close to Wes, rubbing his right hand over Wes's arm. Wes shivered, not in anticipation, but in disgust. Before Wes could say anything, Kieran lifted his other hand and snapped a photo of them with his phone. "Memories to treasure," he said with a laugh.

Wes grabbed Kieran's arm and hauled him over to the exit doors near the stage. "I have no interest in seeing you. In fact, I would rather forget you even exist. You need to leave, now, or I will have security escort you out. It's your choice." Wes's words were clipped with anger. "And delete that photo before I break your phone."

Kieran's tinny laugh echoed in the doorway. "I forgot what a he-man you are when you get riled up. So feisty, babe. It makes me hot." He gave Wes a once-over. "You're still not over me, are you, Wesley?" Kieran's brown eyes narrowed, searching Wes's face. "You can't handle knowing the man at that table wanted me and there was nothing you could do about it."

Wes laughed, shaking his head. "I don't know what you've been drinking or smoking, but I don't care what you do. Fuck every man in this room. I. Don't. Care. You're a leech looking for his next victim. Get lost before I have you arrested for harassment," Wes spat out as Kieran's face morphed from haughty amusement to a clenched, bitter scowl.

"I'll leave now, but this isn't over." Kieran

sneered and sauntered through the exit door. "You owe me, Wesley."

"I gave you everything, and you betrayed me by trying to sell my private information to the tabloids. I owe you nothing," Wesley shouted after him, his stomach clenching with revulsion, before he headed back into the ballroom.

Willing his body to calm down, Wes texted Luca and Grey to give them a heads-up. Kieran was up to something, and Wes wanted to know what.

Then he texted Ryker.

Wes: **Hey, what are you up to, love?**

Ryker: **Late-night Chinese food with Cal, chatting about his upcoming exhibit and his latest adventure at one of NYC's secret sex clubs. Well, not so secret anymore. You know, the usual. How about you? Aren't you at some fancy dinner tonight?**

Wes: **Yes, but I lost my appetite. Sex club? I hope he has good health insurance.**

Ryker: **LOL, he also buys stock in Trojan condoms. So, what happened to make you lose your appetite?**

Wes: **Some guy I can't stand showed up uninvited and I had to kick him out. He's a parasite.**

Ryker: **Sounds dramatic. Are you okay?**

Wes: **Yup just needed to chat with my boyfriend.**

Ryker: **Well, I'd better let you go so you can do that.** □

Wes: **Has anyone told you that you're adorable?**

Ryker: **No one. Grumpy? Moody? Sarcastic? Yup. Adorable? Nope.**

Wes: **You are. Can I call you later? I miss your voice.**

Ryker: **I'll be waiting.**

Wes: **xoxo**

Ryker: ☐

Feeling much lighter, Wes sat down at his table and apologized to the guests for the earlier drama. He introduced himself, absorbing the friendly chatter and lively music around him as his anger slowly faded away.

****

Ryker

After copious amounts of Chinese food and beer, Ryker and Cal took Spock for a late-night walk around the block. The air was warm and breezy and filled with the sounds of cars rushing by and pedestrians chatting away as they strolled along the sidewalk. Ryker was comfortable in his t-shirt and jeans, but Cal tightened his blue denim jacket around his body as if he were cold.

"You haven't mentioned anything about the weird text messages, so I assume they've stopped?" Ryker asked as they watched Spock sniff every inch of the sidewalk around them.

"Yup, thank God that's over with. It was probably a sick joke. You know, someone I slept with who was pissed at me for not calling or something."

Cal shrugged, and Ryker took a moment to look over his friend. There were dark circles under his eyes, and he seemed distracted. Cal never wanted to burden others with his problems, and despite his usually happy demeanor, he was prone to the occasional bout of depression, and Ryker had witnessed firsthand how quickly things could spiral.

"You look tired. Too many late nights?" Ryker inquired gently.

"Yeah, I've been working long hours in my studio, and then I went out twice this week. I can't believe I'm saying this, but I think I'm getting too old for so many late nights. And the party scene is starting to bore me. I've been feeling kinda restless lately. Nothing satisfies. And ever since the night of Mac's party, I can't stop thinking about him, which is strange." As if suddenly realizing he was voicing his comments out loud, Cal closed his mouth and ran a hand through his hair. He paced back and forth on the sidewalk, shaking his head.

"Him? Have you met someone?" Ryker asked.

Cal paused for a moment, then resumed his pacing. Ryker said nothing, but he noticed Cal's jaw clench.

Ryker didn't want to push his friend to talk, but it was clear that something was on his mind. "You know you can tell me anything, right? We've all been through some heavy shit, and I'm always here if you need to vent."

Cal grinned. "I know. It's funny, I thought I knew who I was and what I wanted out of life. I've always been content to be impulsive and never tied down to one person. Except for my friends—you and Mac—of course. But I look at how happy you seem now that Wes is in your life, and I wonder if maybe I'm missing out on something. Anyway, it's probably just a weird phase I'm going through. Ignore me." Cal smiled halfheartedly.

"Who is this man you can't stop thinking about?"

Ryker's question was met with silence for a moment. "No one, never mind. I'm not made for anything long term. You know me. Guy or girl, I like them all." Cal winked and bent down to pet Spock, who gleefully got up on his hind legs to lick Cal's hand.

"You never know. If grumpy me can find love, there's hope for everyone else," Ryker mused as his friend lifted Spock into his arms.

"So, you admit that you love Wes." Cal smiled as they walked back to Ryker's apartment building.

"Yup, I haven't said the words to him yet, but I feel it. As crazy as it sounds, after such a short time, it happened. I never believed it when people talked about love at first sight, but I can now tell you that it's true." Ryker slung his arm over Cal's shoulders. "One down, two to go. Let's see, who will be the next victim to fall prey to love in the Big Apple? You or Mac? Place your bets," Ryker said with a chuckle.

"Who are you and what have you done with Ryker?" Cal laughed and shook his head. "It's not gonna be me. Never gonna happen so save your money. Ain't no man brave or stupid enough to take on my brand of crazy."

"I don't know. I think there may be a calm, sophisticated guy out there brave enough to complement your wild nature," Ryker said as Cal pretended to gag.

Ryker checked his phone as they entered the building. He'd missed Wes's call an hour ago. Shit.

"I've gotta head back up and call Wes." Ryker motioned to the elevators.

"I'm off," Cal said. He placed Spock in Ryker's arms. "I'm gonna head home and sleep for two days straight. Thanks for the Chinese food and the talk." Cal hugged Ryker.

"Anytime. About anything. I mean it, bud." Cal nodded and headed out.

Ryker hopped into the elevator. As soon as he got back to his apartment, he unleashed Spock and dialed Wes.

On the fourth ring, the voice of a man that Ryker did not recognize answered. "Hello?"

"Hey, can I speak to Wes, please?" Ryker asked, finding it odd that someone other than Wes would answer his cell, especially at one in the morning.

"I'm sorry, he's in the shower. You'll have to try

again another day," the smooth voice said.

"But he's expecting my call. My name is Ryker and…"

The smooth voice lowered. "I don't care who you are. You're interrupting us, and he doesn't want to be disturbed. Don't call back."

And with that, Ryker was left staring at his phone in confusion.

Interrupting what? No. He wouldn't lie to me. That's not Wes. Not after everything we just talked about. But someone was answering Wes's phone while he was in the shower at one in the morning. What the fuck was going on?

Mac's comments from the other day rushed to the surface of his mind. What if he'd been right and Wes was hooking up with some random guy? Wes had lots of opportunity, after all. *What if he's just playing a game with me?* It felt like a weight was crushing Ryker's chest the more he thought about the situation. This was why he preferred one-night stands. Relationships were messy and painful and way too complicated to navigate. It had taken his mom years to get over his father's abandonment. No way did Ryker want to find himself in the same situation, investing all his love and attention in Wes only to have him smash his heart to bits and leave him devastated. *Jesus.*

Ryker grabbed his headphones and blasted Linkin Park. The loud, angry rock music helped his mind recalibrate. Had he made a terrible mistake trusting his heart to Wes?

Over an hour later, his phone rang.

Ryker refused to look at it.

Chapter Twenty-Four
Wes

Wes was fucking exhausted. From the pre-dinner soap opera with Kieran to the late-night dancing, he'd finally begged off just after midnight, needing a hot shower and a warm bed. Under the pounding spray of the rainfall shower, Wes's muscles relaxed and his mind cleared. He would call Ryker quickly and then tumble into bed for much-needed sleep.

Slipping into the plush hotel bathrobe, Wes stepped out of the marble bathroom and into his bedroom.

"Hello, Wesley," a voice greeted him in the dark.

"Jesus!" Wes flicked on the bedside lamp and found Kieran stretched out on his bed. Completely naked. "What the hell are you doing in my hotel room? Have you totally lost your mind? How did you get in here?" Wes yelled.

Kieran just smiled. "I told the front desk that I was your husband and couldn't find my key. And then I slipped the assistant manager two hundred bucks. You'd be surprised how easily hotel staff can be bribed." He laughed. "Come on, I know you miss me. No one fucks like I do, right, baby?"

Wes grabbed the clothes lying on the floor and tossed them at Kieran, then walked over to the bedside and picked up the phone.

"This is Wes Stewart in the penthouse suite. I want to speak to the manager. Now!" He paused. "I don't give a shit what time it is. One of your staff let someone into my room, without my permission, invading my privacy. Now you either call the police and get your manager up here, or I will!" Wes slammed down the phone and grabbed Kieran by the arm, shoving him toward the door. "I'm pressing charges against you. Don't ever contact me again. *Out!*"

Wes opened the door and threw the clothes, and a nude Kieran, into the hallway, not giving a shit who saw the spectacle. Several other doors opened, and curious guests popped their heads out, their faces either shocked or amused when they caught sight of the naked man.

"Wait, wait! Wes, I need a couple thousand dollars. I got kicked out of my last place. The old fucker I lived with cut me off. Come on, you owe me."

Wes slammed and locked the door, ignored Kieran's banging and wailing. Eight minutes later, the police arrived along with the manager, and Wes gave his full account. Kieran was finally allowed to get dressed and was escorted out of the building. The hotel offered to comp everything if Wes didn't sue, and since he was still a nice Canadian guy, he agreed. He was too tired to care at this point.

When everyone had left, Wes checked his phone. No text, voicemail, or missed calls from Ryker. Then he checked his call log. Ryker had called at one twelve AM. The call had lasted for one minute and ten seconds.

Wait. Wes hadn't talked to Ryker, and that was over an hour ago, when he was in the shower.

Oh, fuck.

Wes dialed Ryker. Voicemail. Again, voicemail. *Shit.*

"It's me, please, please call me back. My crazy ex bribed his way into my hotel room. I had him arrested. I just finished talking to the police. I don't know what he said to you, but it's total bullshit. Nothing happened. I kicked him out as soon as I saw him. Please call me back," Wes pleaded.

He sat down slowly on his bed, leaned back against the headboard, and closed his eyes.

The warmth of the shower was long gone, replaced by a cold awareness that had nothing to do with the temperature and everything to do with the fear that Ryker wouldn't call him back.

****

Ryker

Love sucked. And not in the good way.

Ryker tossed and turned for most of the night, unable to sleep, and finally rolled out of bed at six thirty AM. He went through his usual routine: walk Spock, feed the beasts, make coffee, eat food, work, check his e-mail, all the while ignoring his phone. He knew he couldn't put it off forever and was being dramatic, so he finally sat down around noon and listened to Wes's voicemail.

Ryker knew in his heart that Wes was telling the truth. That wasn't the issue. The incident had, however, made Ryker aware of how quickly he'd become invested in Wes, how much it might hurt if—when—things ended. He'd always avoided intimate relationships for that very reason. His mother had been so stricken when his father left, it was like she'd grieved his death. Even when he was a little boy, years after his father's departure, Ryker would sometimes find her crying in her bedroom, repeating his name. He knew he never wanted to go through that kind of pain. And opening his heart to Wes would mean he'd have to face that possibility. Maybe it was already too late.

Was he strong enough?

Ryker could admit he was in love. But was he ready for this relationship? The reality was, they lived in two different countries. How would the long-distance thing work? And what about Wes's penchant for publicity? Would he want their private life posted all over social media? Ryker needed time to figure out what he was able to give and how much he was willing to take.

Ryker: **I got your voicemail. I believe you. I'm sorry you had to go through that. I just need some time to myself and will contact you soon, I promise.**

Wes: **Okay. I miss you. Please reach out to me, day or night.**

He was relieved that Wes hadn't pushed him to get on the phone, like he'd instinctively known Ryker would be skittish at the first sign of relationship trouble. As it turned out, the crazy ex was just the beginning. The next morning, Ryker stepped out with Spock for his usual walk, only to be ambushed by reporters in front of his building.

"Ryker Desoumas!"

"Over here!"

"You were seen with Wes Stewart at a coffee shop early Thursday morning. Are you two an item? How did you meet?"

Between the camera flashes and the yelling, Ryker's anxiety took over, and he ran as fast as he could to get away from whoever was following him. He managed to yell "No comment" and kept going, lifting Spock into his arms to protect him. Fuck, this was just the type of thing he hated—and why he never publicized who he was. Now that he was with Wes, was this going to be his life?

An hour later, Ryker returned to his building and managed to get back inside without incident. He advised the concierge about the reporters, called his agent, and notified Mac to be on guard, but Mac just shrugged it off.

"I'm used to it, Ry. New York paparazzi don't faze me much at all. They've been following my family for decades. You shouldn't be bothered either. You know what it's like."

"Sure, I was on the other side of the story years

ago, but I never harassed people about who they were dating. This personal shit, it's so invasive," Ryker muttered.

"You might as well make peace with the fact that today, everyone is watching your every move. It's not just the press. Anyone with a smartphone acts like they're the paparazzi now. Just keep living your life and don't let them get to you. Once they find another celebrity to follow, they'll leave Wes, and you, alone."

"They haven't left you alone," Ryker pointed out.

"That's because I'm the outcast of the well-connected Duran clan. They're waiting for my downfall or a public family feud. Trust me, you're just the flavor of the day. The newness will wear off quickly."

"I don't know. They seem to follow Wes a lot, and he seems to court them. I need to talk to him about all this. Anyway, I have to do something to get rid of all my angsty energy. Thanks for the talk, Mac."

Next, Ryker dialed Cal. "Hey, are you busy?"

"Nope. What's up?"

"Other than Wes's crazy ex following him, and the paparazzi following me because of him, not much." Ryker sighed, exasperated by today's turn of events. "I'm headed to my Krav Maga class. You want to join? I could use the company."

"Is your instructor hot?" Cal asked.

"I don't know! Is that all you think about?" Ryker growled, pacing back and forth.

"Whoa, easy. I was just teasing. Of course I'll go with you. Tell me when and where."

"Sorry, it's been a shitty twenty-four hours and I need a release. Pick me up in twenty. The studio is in Tribeca."

"You got it."

Two hours later, they were both sweaty and out of

breath and taking a much-needed cool down. Ryker had been training for a decade and was comfortable practicing with the senior members of the school. Cal, on the other hand, had gotten his ass kicked by a lady half his size and three times his age, much to the amusement of the entire class.

"Shit, this stuff is hard, man. That lady nearly fed me my balls," Cal said as he bent over, gasping for breath. "I'm not having any fun. Please tell me there's a naked version of this later on with hot people."

Ryker laughed and wiped the sweat from his face and neck with a large towel. "Nope, sorry. I thought you'd be in better shape with all the sex you supposedly have. You're getting old."

"No fucking way! I'm just tired from too many late nights. And what do you mean, 'supposedly'? Definitely! I just need more sleep. Next time, I'll be ready to kick ass." Cal grinned.

"I think they've decided to put you in the kids' group instead." Ryker chuckled, and Cal threw his towel at him.

"Come on, now that we've expended all our aggressive energy, let's grab some food and drink," Cal suggested, and they left to do just that.

Later on, at home, Ryker soaked in his large copper tub and let the bath salts ease his aching muscles. The exercise had drained him of all his anxiety, leaving him feeling calm and empowered, like he did after every workout. It didn't matter that he wasn't the strongest, the tallest, or the biggest fighter. Self-defense gave him the confidence that he could face whatever physical and mental conflict lay ahead.

It was the emotional conflict he was still unsure about.

Ryker sighed and called the one person he could

count on for objective advice.

"Hey, it's me again."

"What's up?" Mac replied.

"It's about Wes."

"What about him?"

"I have more on my mind than just the tabloid reporters who followed me today. Wes had an incident the other night with a crazy ex, and it freaked me out. All of a sudden, I realized how much I cared about him and how easily I could get hurt. You're right. We live far apart, so how's that gonna work? Maybe I should let go of him before I get in too deep."

"Look, I'll be the first to admit that when you told us about the two of you a week ago, I was not entirely supportive. Especially given your new working partnership. I've never seen you take any interest in a long-term relationship, and suddenly, you jumped in headfirst. I'm sorry, but I was worried about you." He paused. "Having said that, you can't be afraid of getting hurt. Sorry, but that's life. And there are no guarantees with anything. You love Wes, don't you?"

"I haven't said those exact words to him yet, but yes."

"You trust him?"

"Yup."

"Then what is there to talk about? Life is fucking short, Ry. You don't want to wake up one day and realize that you only have your work to fulfill you. That despite attending dinner parties and social events, you sit alone in your office until ten at night, night after night, wondering what it would be like to come home to someone special. You will probably, inevitably, get hurt, but you'll also feel more alive than you ever have before."

"I know," Ryker said quietly. "Thanks, Mac."

"No worries, but I have to get back to work. I

have contracts to negotiate."

"Okay, I'll let you get back to it. I have a plane to book."

This time, it was Wes's turn for a surprise.

Chapter Twenty-Five
Wes

It was the beginning of June, and Wes was finally home.

His plane landed at the Toronto Island Airport at eight in the evening, the sun hanging low and painting the sky with streaks of pink and orange. Lake Ontario shimmered on the horizon as he stepped off the plane and onto the tarmac.

A short ride later, he was back home in the Beaches, a waterfront community in the east end of the city that was known for its two-mile boardwalk and sandy dunes. Wes took in the changes that had occurred over the past month. The trees and gardens had fully bloomed, and there were new billboards for the annual jazz festival that drew tens of thousands of visitors every July. The low-rise shops and restaurant patios dotting Queen Street were packed with people.

Wes had never felt so alone.

His car turned on Balric Avenue and up the long gravel driveway to his house. He'd bought the two-story brick home a decade ago, captivated by the private frontage, outdoor pool, and rooftop deck that looked out over the lake. Easing out of the car, he grabbed his bags and sauntered up to the front door. He entered his security passcode and dropped his bags in the foyer. The familiar click of doggy toenails on the hardwood floor greeted him. Luca had kindly dropped off Peanut and Rudy in advance, knowing Wes needed his fur babies after so many weeks away.

"Peanut, how are you? I've missed you." Wes crouched down and hugged his five-year-old Labrador-husky mix. Rudy, the dog Wes had adopted from New

York, wandered over slowly, still a bit hesitant until he got closer. "Rudy, how's my newest baby?" Wes cooed.

Peanut and Rudy wagged their tails excitedly as they jumped and licked Wes, and he savored the affection. He immediately thought of Spock and imagined how all three dogs would get along—not to mention Ryker's cats—if they all lived together.

If there was still a *together* to wonder over.

Wes agreed to give Ryker his space, since he knew his man, knew him pretty damn well even though they'd only met a month ago. Ryker was retreating, thinking of all the pros and cons to this relationship, wondering how it would all work out, trying to rationalize feelings that didn't make sense on paper but only to the heart.

For the time being, Wes would do what he needed to do. Rest, play with his dogs, hit the beach, and meet up with friends. Relax and recharge. Then he would fly to New York and convince the man he loved that he was worth a second shot.

****

Ryker

Ryker found himself at La Guardia Airport, his mood souring by the minute. How the fuck did Wes travel so much and still remain a positive person? The hordes of people, the long lines, the waiting, the hordes of people.

Ryker got up and paced. Several passengers in the first-class departure lounge got out of his way when they saw the expression on his face. *Maybe turn the scowl down a notch or two.* It probably didn't help that he wore his usual black outfit of jeans and a t-shirt, with dark sunglasses and a leather motorcycle jacket, his long hair loose and his face badly in need of a shave. Someone in the seat nearby mumbled something about traveling with cranky rockstars, and Ryker couldn't help but let out a low laugh.

He stopped pacing and slid into a leather chair, checking his phone again for any updates from Luca.

Two days ago, Luca had kindly agreed to help Ryker with his surprise visit to Toronto, taking care of all the details that Ryker hadn't thought of and that made him want to rip his hair out. Luca was clearly in love with love and had been all too happy to arrange a surprise dinner date for Wes, *ooh-ing* and *ahh-ing* over Ryker's suggestion.

"You know, I have to give Mac credit for all this," Ryker had said as he FaceTimed with Luca.

"What do you mean?"

"He told me to take a chance. That I might end up hurt but to follow my heart anyway. The tough negotiator has a soft side. Don't tell him I said so," Ryker warned.

Luca paused. "No worries there. Who would have guessed the Ice Man had feelings? But you know him better than I do. Controlling, uptight workaholic. The way he barked orders at me when we were getting your book deal finalized, let me tell you, I just wanted to reach through the laptop and yank on his tie. Shit, I'm sorry. I know he's your friend, but the man infuriates me like no one else." Luca finished his rant, and Ryker let it be. He was all too aware of the growing tension between Luca and Mac, and in no way did he want to get involved in their hot-tempered drama.

Ryker's flight was called, and a short hour and a half later, he landed at a small airport just south of the city. He checked in to the Kings Hotel's executive suite and dropped his bags on the garment rack. Normally, he'd take time to shower and shave, but he was too excited to wait.

Ryker: **I'm all checked in. Is the plan in motion?**

Luca: **Yup, your car service will drive you to Harbourfront. Ask for Drummond and you'll be escorted to the boat. I'll make sure your man will be there on time!**

Ryker: **Thanks Luca, I owe you.**

Luca: **Invite me to the bachelor party.**

****

Wes

"What is the fucking rush, Luca?" Wes barked as he was shoved out the door of his own house. He was in a shitty mood, and Luca forcing him to head downtown to some high-octane event tonight was not helping. Despite the sunny spring evening, Wes wanted to wallow in his misery and loneliness. *Jesus, dramatic much?*

Three more days had gone by without a word from Ryker, and it was driving Wes nuts. He couldn't eat or sleep. He missed Ryker's quiet, solid presence in his life—their late-night marathon phone calls, and silly, often sappy, text messages. Wes had finally met someone who understood him, someone that saw beyond the persona to the real man underneath, only to have him pull away.

Wes missed Ryker so much that he'd dreamed of them together, and when he woke this morning, he could have sworn he smelled Ryker's distinctive scent in his room. He'd also woken with a raging hard-on, but he didn't bother to pleasure himself. The body wanted, but the heart and brain were not cooperating, so he'd taken a cold shower and gotten on with his day. He wrote furiously for several hours, using all his pent-up energy on something he could control. He completed a couple of chapters and vowed to send them off to Ryker tomorrow for his input. Then maybe he'd get some sort of communication from his silent partner.

But for now, Luca was determined to get him out of his house and back to normal living, including socializing.

"Okay, all right! I'm going. What is your problem? You're even more hyper than usual," Wes whined as he was marched to the passenger door of his red Porsche.

"It's called energy, Wes. Remember that? You had some a few months ago, but now you're sad and hiding in your home like a big baby," Luca said, slipping into the leather driving seat, buckling his seat belt, and revving up the engine.

"I'm not hiding. I'm resting! I've had a stressful month!" Wes yelled, crossing his arms and pursing his lips.

Luca turned slowly in the driver's seat to face Wes and lowered his large designer sunglasses down his nose. "Wes, I know you. You miss Ryker, and you want to wallow in your misery. But that won't help. You're hurt, not dead. And he will call you back. He just needs some time. So buckle up and put on your happy face. We're going to have a good time tonight!"

Luca grabbed the gearshift and shot down the driveway. Wes suddenly remembered that Luca drove like a maniac, and he white-knuckled it all the way downtown. Twenty harrowing minutes later, they exited Lakeshore Drive onto Front Street.

"So, where are we going?" Wes finally asked, a little bit of his natural curiosity waking up again.

"It's a fundraising event on a yacht at the Harbourfront marina. Dinner and dancing and a tour of the lake. Just what you need to take your mind off you-know-who," Luca said, weaving in and out of traffic at an alarming rate until he found a parking spot. Luca slammed on the brakes and shifted into park.

"Jesus, next time I'll grab stomach meds for the drive in, never mind the boat ride," Wes moaned.

Luca rolled his eyes and got out of the car. Wes followed, the wind blowing his hair in every direction as they walked over to the marina and down the dock. Boats of varying shapes and sizes bobbed in the water, with people onboard laughing and chatting and celebrating an early summer evening. Wes took a deep breath to appreciate the moment and decided to make the most of the evening.

Wes and Luca walked to the end of the last pier, where a large fifty-foot beauty called *Smooth Sailing* was docked. Wes didn't notice anyone on or around the boat, save for someone at the helm. Had they arrived too early?

"Luca, are you sure this is the right boat? There doesn't seem to be anyone here yet," Wes said as he raised his sunglasses to get a better look at the yacht and their surroundings.

"This is the one. You head on in. I need to talk to the charter captain," Luca said as he waved at the man on the top deck.

Wes stepped onto the boat, but he didn't see a single person on the lower deck. He walked over to the door to the cabin and opened it, peering inside to find a large lounge area with two sofas and a coffee table. Beyond that, a dining room and bar and a galley kitchen. As he stepped inside, he noticed soft music playing.

Wes wandered through, noting that the dining table was set for two, with tiny lanterns creating a warm glow. *We must be on the wrong boat*, he thought as he started to head back outside to find Luca. But just as he turned, he caught sight of someone entering from the galley.

AVA OLSEN

"Hey, Prince Charming."

Chapter Twenty-Six
Ryker

Ryker was so nervous, he wanted to puke. Or maybe that was the motion of the boat. Either way, he couldn't wait until Wes got here.

Everything was set for the evening. Now he just needed his man.

Ryker watched from the small galley as Wes entered the lounge, his blond hair ruffled by the wind, his face tired but beautiful. He looked like he hadn't shaved for a few days, and there were dark circles under his eyes. Ryker felt a pang of regret that he may have caused Wes sleepless nights. He took in Wes's slim dark jeans and white button-down shirt with the sleeves casually rolled up, his strong forearms on display. Ryker was once again blown away by the powerful feelings this man evoked, all of his senses lighting up again in his presence. It was time to let Wes know how much he loved him and hope for the best.

Ryker saw Wes's look of confusion as he peered at the dining table, then pivoted to head back out to the deck. Before Wes made it to the door, Ryker entered the room.

"Hey, Prince Charming," he greeted Wes. A nod to the night at Mac's when they'd stood together on the rooftop patio under the stars. Back to where it all began.

Wes turned slowly, his hands tucked into his jean pockets, his hazel eyes warm and glowing. Ryker felt his heart expand and his body flush with heat.

"It's about time you woke up, Sleeping Beauty," Wes said, smiling.

Ryker rushed over and cupped Wes's face, leaning in and sealing their lips in a kiss that was urgent and sweet and so fierce that they both trembled. The kiss went on and on, their lips and tongues tangling together in their need to get as close as physically possible, to claim each other in the most primal way. Wes ran his hands up Ryker's back, across his neck, and over Ryker's hands, joining them and gripping tightly. Ryker took a deep breath. The familiar scents of salt and citrus hit him, and he pulled back slightly, looking deep into Wes's eyes and seeing the undeniable love mirrored back at him.

"I love you," Ryker said for the first time as he took Wes's lips again, nipping gently, then pouring everything he had into the kiss. "I'm sorry I had a freak-out moment. I love you and want to be with you, and I promise I'm all in," he murmured, his eyes filling up with the surge of emotion he could not control.

Wes smiled even wider as his eyes roamed Ryker's face. "I love you, too. So much, Ry. Fuck, we've only been apart a short period of time and it feels like years. Don't shut me out again. Please, love."

Ry whispered his reply: "No, never."

They stood together tightly, shaking and crying and kissing. Ryker was ready and so was his heart.

****

Wes

His man was here, and Wes was never letting him go.

When Ryker walked out of the galley and called to him, Wes felt his heart stop. And then he turned around, and the impact of Ryker's presence was just as powerful as the first time they'd met. Ryker was wearing his usual black outfit, this time with a leather jacket. His long hair was loose, tumbling over his shoulders in dark, silky waves that were begging for Wes's touch. But it was those big blue eyes, the ones that had called to him from the very beginning, that were Wes's undoing. He could see the love shining in them before Ryker uttered the words.

And when they kissed, fuck, what a kiss. Ryker's rough beard sparked the sensitive nerves around Wes's mouth, and his spicy flavor was warm and sensuous. He tasted like the only kiss Wes craved, and he would never get enough.

After their mutual declarations of love, Ryker motioned to the couch. Ryker poured two glasses of champagne and handed one to Wes.

"I know we have a lot to talk about, but first, a toast. To our amazing, unexpected partnership—the best gift I never saw coming. To us, love," Ryker murmured and leaned forward to kiss him.

"To us, sweetheart," Wes repeated as they clinked their glasses together.

"As you probably guessed by know, Luca had a hand in planning this surprise," Ryker said as he settled on the couch beside Wes, draping his arm over the back of the sofa and around Wes's shoulders. "The boat ride was my idea, but Luca made it happen. That man is scary organized." Ryker laughed as he sipped the champagne.

"Yes, he is. Remind me to give him a bonus," Wes said.

Ryker paused and took a deep breath. "I'm sorry for pulling back on you. I got overwhelmed for a while. First, the phone call with your ex, and then reporters hounded me after you left, and I just needed some time to myself."

"I'm sorry, Ry. I can't say for sure that the press won't be an issue. I don't want to spend my life in a fishbowl anymore, but there will still be events and public appearances."

"I know. After I calmed down, I was able to see

that our relationship will mean big changes for both of us. Some may be difficult to navigate, but many of them will be great. And I want them all. I'm ready for them." Ryker leaned in and rubbed his nose into Wes's hair.

"I'm ready for them, too. I still can't believe you're here."

"Believe it, love. So, the one question that remains is, did you manage to get rid of your nasty ex? I don't want to spoil the mood, but we should probably talk about it," Ryker said.

"I got rid of him. For now. But his lawyer bailed him out. I filed a restraining order yesterday. Kieran is a manipulative asshole, so there's no telling what he might do."

"Tell me about that night in Portland. What happened?"

"Keiran showed up at the dinner I was attending. I kicked him out, but he followed me back to my hotel. He bribed an employee to let him into my room. He just needs money. Once he finds a new sugar daddy, he'll go away, but fuck, what a crazy mess."

Ryker massaged Wes's shoulders, releasing the tension there. "I'm sorry you had to go through that. He sounds like a piece of work. Do you mind if I ask how you met and what happened between you?"

"We met three and a half years ago. I was attending a restaurant opening, and he was working as a waiter. He was young and hot, and latched on to my every word, so of course I was flattered. And he told me he wanted to be a writer and asked if I could help him. Stupid me, I believed him." He shook his head.

"One month later, he moved in with me, and then the real Kieran Moore appeared. He quit his job but didn't look for another one, and there was always some excuse why he couldn't find work. He ran up huge credit card debts, which I'd pay off. We'd be at parties and he would disappear, and then I'd find out he was fucking one person or another. But I thought I loved him, so I forgave him.

"Anyway, the final straw came when I noticed some of my personal journals missing a few months later. He'd contacted the tabloids to sell select content in return for a tidy sum. I heard him on the phone when I came home early one day, so I threw him out of the house. Because of our very busy social life, he was quick to find another rich man to sucker. That's his MO." Wes sighed.

"And then you swore off relationships," Ryker murmured, moving his hands up to Wes's neck and scalp, rubbing and touching softly as Wes moaned his appreciation.

"Yup. Until I met this hot, moody author who rocked my world." Wes turned and was met with the beauty of Ryker's biggest smile, so potent it made Wes's breath catch. Would it always have that effect on him?

Ryker leaned forward and kissed him again, obliterating all thoughts, worries, and fears. Wes didn't want to think, or talk about, Kieran anymore. The past was over. It was time to focus on the future.

"Before I forget," Ryker said as he pulled a small, black velvet bag from his jacket. "I have a gift for you." He placed the bag in Wes's hand.

Wes slowly opened the drawstring bag and removed a bracelet similar to the one Ryker wore, except this one had brown beads with golden striations.

"These beads are tiger's eye. The color reminded me of your eyes," Ryker said quietly and slipped the bracelet onto Wes's wrist. "They're supposed to encourage feelings of empowerment and offer protection."

Wes rubbed the bracelet and slowly reached up to

cup Ryker's face. "It's perfect. I love it," he said. "Come on. Let's head up on deck and watch the sunset. We have a night on the water to enjoy," Wes murmured against Ryker's lips. "Then I want to show you my home."

They made their way to the upper deck and greeted the charter captain, who was readying the boat launch for the lake tour. Wes pulled Ryker in close as they leaned against the deck railing, enjoying the view of the cityscape set in full relief against the pink-hued sky. They waved at nearby sailboats and water taxis as they left the marina.

"Let's grab dinner and eat out here," Wes suggested.

They did just that and enjoyed more champagne with their dinner, which included ribeye steaks with salad and a rich chocolate cheesecake for dessert. When neither of them could eat any more, they sat close together and chatted, enjoying the uninterrupted time together. Several hours passed and the sky darkened, the full moon high above reflected in the water. The lack of clouds and their distance from the city lights allowed for stargazing. Sitting together on a lounger, the sparkling vision above them reminded Wes of the tattoo on Ryker's back.

"The tattoo between your shoulder blades—with the moon and the blazing comet—is there a special meaning behind it? I meant to ask weeks ago, but I guess I got distracted by the rest of your body." Wes smirked and hugged Ryker closer, kissing the top of his head.

"I've always been fascinated with astronomy and space. Mom took us to the Hayden Planetarium when we were kids, and I was hooked. I guess that's why when I turned to creative writing, I focused on science fiction. I sometimes have a hard time dealing with people in real life, but in the worlds I create, everything makes sense to me. I'm free from limitations. I got the tattoo a year after the assault incident. It was important to me to have a reminder that no matter what happens in my life, I'll persevere with passion and purpose." He paused. "Hey, did you know comets can spend thousands of years in the solar system before they return to the sun? But they always return," Ryker murmured, staring up at Wes with eyes as dark as the sky.

"Are you saying you'll always come back to me?" Wes asked.

"Always."

No more words were needed after that.

Chapter Twenty-Seven
Ryker

Ryker spent the rest of the week at Wes's home, and both Peanut and Rudy took to him like long lost pals. The week was full of walks on the beach, dinners with Wes's friends—including Grey and Luca—and a video call with Ryker's sister, Rachel. But the majority of time was spent in bed, touching, talking, and laughing. Ryker was afraid the neighbors might show up to complain after a rather noisy round of sex in the outdoor pool late one night, but Wes wasn't worried.

"They're used to my sexy antics," he'd joked as they left the pool.

"As long as I'm the only one you do sexy antics with from now on," Ryker had replied, swatting Wes hard on his bare, wet ass, then running inside to avoid retaliation as Wes chased him through the house. The dogs watched the crazy humans in confusion.

The only blip came halfway during his stay when Wes's ex showed up. A yelling match ensued on the driveway, and Wes was about to call the cops before Ryker intervened.

"Wes, go inside. I'm going to talk to Kieran alone."

"Ry, I don't think that's a good idea."

"Five minutes. Trust me," Ryker pleaded, and finally, Wes nodded. Wes walked back up his driveway and into the house. Once Ryker saw the door close, he turned back to Kieran.

Ryker gave Kieran his coldest glare. "So, Kieran, here's what's going to happen. I'm going to give you a business card." Ryker paused and pulled out several cards from his pocket. He searched through them and found the one he was looking for, a thick red card that had been burning a hole in his pocket for over a month now. He was glad to get rid of it. "You're going to call the number on it next week. The number belongs to a very, very wealthy man who I'm sure would be happy to befriend you. You're going to obey the restraining order and never, ever contact Wes again. Are we clear?"

Kieran's model-worthy pout screwed up tight as he looked Ryker over. "How wealthy?" he asked.

"Ten times wealthier than Wes," Ryker replied calmly.

Kieran took a long look at the card and finally nodded. "Okay. But this better pan out."

Ryker nodded in return. "Now it's time for you to leave," he said, escorting Kieran to the end of the driveway, where his car was parked. Ryker watched until Kieran got in the car and sped off out of sight, and then he headed back inside to find his man.

"I can't believe he left! What did you say to him?" Wes asked.

"Hold on, sweetheart, I have a phone call to make."

Ryker picked up his cell. "Harrison? It's Ryker Desoumas. Yes, it has been a while since Mac's party. No, no, thanks, I have a boyfriend. Look, I gave your card to a man named Kieran Moore. Late twenties, looks like a pouty GQ model, with an attitude to match. He's looking for a sugar daddy, but he's not trustworthy. I wanted to warn you he'll be in touch. Sorry, but he was hung up on my boyfriend, and I needed a diversion." Ryker paused, then burst out laughing. "Yes, okay, have fun," he said before hanging up.

"What is going on, Ry?" Wes asked, shaking his head in confusion.

"Remember Harrison Ruehl from Mac's party?

The guy who was sitting beside me?"

"Yes," Wes grumbled. "He had his hands all over you. I wanted to rip his head off."

"I love your caveman attitude." Ryker laughed. "Anyway, it suddenly occurred to me: He's an obscenely rich sugar daddy, always looking for his next playmate, and Kieran fits the bill perfectly. When we were at Mac's, Harrison slipped his card into my pocket. I forgot about it until I was preparing for my trip up here."

Wes glared at him. "Relax, love, it's not like that. I brought the card with me to give to Luca. Harrison is a big deal, and I thought I could send some event business Luca's way and repay him for organizing my surprise visit. So, that's the story. But I wanted to warn Harrison first about Kieran's behavior. I'm not going to screw him over completely, because he's more or less a decent guy. Really fucking pushy, but decent.

"And Harrison is looking forward to meeting Kieran. He said, 'Thanks, I'm always up for fun and games, and I'll thoroughly enjoy teaching my new pet some important lessons.'"

"What the hell does that mean?" Wes asked.

"It means he'll likely turn the tables on your ex. Kieran thinks he's after some senile sugar daddy when, in fact, Harrison will probably lure him in and then make him work for it." Ryker laughed as Wes stood there with his mouth hanging open.

"I hope your devious plan works," Wes murmured as he slowly ran his hands down Ryker's back and over his ass. "You, my love, are a man of many talents. How can I ever repay you?"

"I can think of several ways," Ryker said, nipping at Wes's smiling lips. "And they all begin with you getting naked."

Wes was more than happy to oblige.

****

Wes

Ryker flew back home the next week and took Wes's heart with him. The house was too quiet, and Wes knew what he had to do next. This week had cemented their relationship, and the step he was about to take would be the right one.

Wes had Luca arrange a charter flight to New York on the fifteenth so that he, Grey, and Luca could all head down to attend the Heart2Home benefit. Then he had some very important shopping to do.

They boarded the flight with relative ease, but Wes was hyped up like a kid before Christmas, much to the amusement and frustration of his nearest and dearest friends. As soon as the seatbelt sign turned off, Wes was up and pacing.

"Will you sit down, have a drink, and relax?" Grey chuckled and handed Wes a vodka on the rocks. "Jesus, I've never seen you so hopped up before. I'm surprised customs let you through."

"Shut up, you're just jealous of my youthful energy." Wes downed the drink in one go and started pacing the cabin again.

Luca rolled his eyes and ran a hand through his now red-tipped hair. "I'm going to make the captain announce that we have to stay seated for the remainder of the flight if you don't stop. This is just an event. You've been to hundreds of them. Why are you so jumpy?"

Wes stopped abruptly and turned to both men.

"I need your help." He paused, then slowly drew a small blue box out of his dress pants.

Luca gasped. "No way! Wes, you're going to propose?" He jumped up to hug Wes, while Grey just sat there with his mouth open.

"I never thought I'd live to see the day. Wes Stewart is getting married. Holy shit!" Grey said, finally getting up and leaning into the group hug.

Wes was suddenly overcome with emotion and tried to regain his composure. "Okay, guys, I need to find a time and place to pop the question. Help me out."

"He'll be receiving an award tonight," Luca blurted out.

"What?"

"When I booked our trip, I contacted the benefit organizers to see if they needed any extra help with the event this evening, and they told me that Ryker will receive a volunteer award for donor of the decade. Maybe you could do it then?"

"I don't know, Ryker doesn't like the spotlight. He may cut and run before I get a chance to get down on one knee," Wes murmured. He started pacing again, running a hand through his hair. "Wait! I've got it!"

"What?" Grey and Luca asked in unison.

"The Hayden Planetarium. His mom took him there as a kid. He's a space junkie. Can you a book a private tour tomorrow?" Wes asked Luca.

"On it," Luca replied.

The captain announced they'd be starting their descent soon. Wes finally sat down and buckled up. Ten minutes later, the plane landed, but Wes's thoughts remained firmly above the clouds.

Chapter Twenty-Eight
Ryker

"Remind me again, why did I agree to go to this event?" Ryker yelled out from his bathroom, adjusting the uncomfortable tie around his neck and fidgeting in his slim tuxedo as he stood in front of the mirror. The black suit was cut perfectly, Ryker thought as he adjusted his lapels and checked himself out. He'd left his long hair loose and decided to wear his contacts tonight, but he'd skipped the eyeliner, much to Wes's disappointment.

"Because you love the shelter and want to show your support," Wes replied, sneaking up behind Ryker and smoothing his hands down his back to rest at his waist. "And because you get to show off your man." Wes winked at him in the mirror and squeezed his waist.

Ryker took a moment to appreciate their profiles in contrast. Wes, bulky and broad, his blond hair and hazel eyes so bright. Ryker, slim but nearly Wes's equal in height, with dark hair and navy-blue eyes. They looked so good together. Ryker's body began to heat up, and his cock swelled in his very tight pants. He reached down to adjust himself. Wes caught the movement, smiled, and dropped a kiss just behind his ear, then moved over to his lobe to lick and gently bite. *Shit.*

"Not there. You know how sensitive I am. I go fucking crazy," Ryker said, wishing they could just stay home instead.

"Sorry, my bad," Wes said and patted his waist. "Come on, we have a party to go to."

He reached out his hand. Ryker interlocked their fingers tightly, never wanting to let go.

They said goodbyes to the fur babies and headed downstairs to their limo. They picked up Grey and Luca and, fifteen minutes later, arrived at Legacy Loft, a well-known venue space in Greenwich Village. The space was over three thousand square feet, with panoramic views of the eclectic neighborhood. The main room was filled with dozens of round tables that each seated eight, decorated in the style of Heart2Home's black, white, and red logo. A DJ was pumping up the large crowd as Ryker searched for his sister and his mom. He spotted them standing by the bar, both dressed in short, stylish cocktail dresses and sipping colorful drinks. Ryker grabbed Wes's hand and tugged him over.

"*Hola, querido*, you look so nice in your tux!" Tina exclaimed, greeting them with hugs. "And you, too, Wes. So handsome."

"Thanks, Tina, but I think Ryker wins for the most beautiful man of the night." Wes chuckled, giving Ryker a once-over. Ryker felt his cheeks heat up.

"Oh, look, Mama, Ryker's blushing," Rachel teased, reaching up and grabbing Ryker's cheek, then turning to greet Wes with a hug. "Wes, it's so nice to meet you in person. The video chat we had when Ryker was visiting you in Toronto was too short." She stood back and looked at both of them. "Wow, you two are stunning together. Can't one of you grow a wart or something?" she joked.

Wes rolled his eyes. "Please, take a look in the mirror. You have lots of men and women glancing your way." Standing tall in a black sequin strapless dress and red satin heels, Rachel Desoumas was a striking beauty, just like her mom and brother. "In fact," Wes said, "you're one amazing family. Let's get some photos."

After pictures and cocktails, Rachel pulled Ryker aside as Wes and Grey wandered over to view the items up for bid in the charity auction.

"I wanted you to know, I submitted my DNA and

got a match a few days ago," she said.

"Holy shit!" Ryker couldn't believe it. "Who did it match to?"

"A first cousin on our father's side. She lives in San Diego. I've reached out to set up a meeting with her when I head to California in August."

Ryker nodded. "Have you told Mom?"

"Yes, and she supports me. I think she'd like answers, too. You know, to finally put everything to rest." Rachel sighed and rubbed her hands together. "I hope that you'll support me, too."

"I'm still getting used to the idea. I may not want to know all the answers just yet, but I'll always love and support you."

Rachel reached up and hugged him. "Thanks, bro. I love you, too."

He squeezed her waist as she drew back.

Ryker then spotted Javier across the room and signaled for him to come over.

"Ryker, so glad you could make it!" Javier said.

Introductions were made, and Wes returned with more drinks.

"Javier, nice to see you again." Wes nodded politely, and Javier shook his hand.

"You traveled a long way for our benefit tonight. Thank you."

"I'm here to support my partner. It's my pleasure," he responded smoothly, sliding his arm around Ryker's waist.

Ryker had a brief flash of guilt when he recalled what he'd said to Javier about not being interested in a relationship. But he'd never be anything more than friends with Javier and had made that clear, so there was nothing to feel guilty about.

Javier looked between Ryker and Wes, then

nodded in understanding. "Wes, I heard you adopted Rudy, congrats. Ryker, Rachel, so nice to chat, but I must go and mingle with potential donors."

Javier headed off into the crowd with the other guests, while Ryker, his family, and Wes found their table. Mac and Cal arrived a few minutes later, and there was a noticeable change in the atmosphere. Mac aimed his icy glare at Luca, and Luca returned it, tenfold. *Great.* Cal and Grey chatted amicably for a while until Cal signaled the waiter for more drinks and downed two glasses of wine in a row.

"Slow down, man, you're going to be shit-faced before the dinner gets started," Ryker whispered.

Cal waved him off, downed another drink, and started flirting with Rachel. Grey abruptly left the table. Ryker looked at Wes, who shrugged.

"He's still out of practice at these things," he said. "He'll be fine."

"So, Big Mac, how's your assistant? Still overworked?" Luca taunted as his glaring match with Mac continued.

Ryker nudged Wes under the table with his knee to get him to defuse the firestorm that was about to erupt.

"She's on vacation, not that it's any of your business," Mac snapped.

"Unlikely. She's at home, on her laptop, job searching," Luca said before turning to Ryker's mother and ignoring Mac's furious scowl.

"Mac, are you having issues with your assistant?" his mom inquired.

"No," Mac replied with a polite smile. "Luca is under the incorrect assumption that she's unhappy and overworked when, in fact, she is well compensated for her hours." Luca opened his mouth to speak, but Ryker's mom beat him to it.

"As a business owner myself, I can tell you that finding—and keeping—good employees is not easy. Don't take them for granted," Tina replied as she sipped her wine.

"Too late," Luca piped in, and Mac's face reddened.

Ryker cleared his throat and decided to change the subject. "So, Mac, Wes and I have completed five chapters. Looks like we'll be on track to have the first draft finished in a few months."

Mac's grimace eased somewhat. "Amazing. How's the move back to fiction, Wes? Any issues?"

"It hasn't been easy, but I have a good beta reader." Wes squeezed Ryker's thigh and leaned in for a kiss. It started out rather chaste, but they soon got lost in each other and forgot about everyone at the table until someone coughed and startled them.

"Enough PDA. Jesus, is it hot in here or is it me?" Cal joked as he tugged on his shirt collar.

"It's just you. You're not used to wearing a shirt." Ryker smirked as everyone at the table laughed.

The lights in the room lowered, and Javier and Charlotte took to the stage with their opening speeches.

Charlotte spoke first. "Thank you again for coming out tonight to support the Heart2Home shelter. I'd like to take this opportunity to thank all our volunteers. A big round of applause, please!" she said as the audience clapped. "And now, I'd like to present our Donor of the Decade award. This is our tenth anniversary, and we could not have been operating for all these years without the support of one very special person. On behalf of the staff and board, I'd like to invite Ryker Desoumas up to the stage to accept this award."

Ryker was in shock. The clapping around him was deafening, and he stood with trembling legs. Wes squeezed his hand and whispered, "Congrats, love." Ryker took a deep breath and made his way to the stage.

He absently accepted the award, a beautiful crystal sculpture, and hugged Charlotte. Then he cleared his throat and bent toward the mic.

"Thank you," he said. "Thank you for this award. Those who know me know that I don't like attention, but I am thankful for your acknowledgment. It means a lot. I've loved animals since I was a kid, and I can't imagine a world without them." He paused and took another deep breath to steady his nerves. "It's true that at the Heart2Home shelter, we rescue animals. But the fact is, they rescue us by loving us unconditionally. Thank you for supporting this benefit and this important cause." And with that, he fled the stage.

Wes stood up at their table. As he came closer, Ryker walked into his arms and hugged him, shuddering in relief and awe that he'd managed to get through his impromptu speech without a major panic attack.

"I'm so proud of you," Wes murmured into his hair, holding on tight. The rest of his family and friends gathered around to offer their congratulations.

An hour later, the party was in full swing. Rachel pulled Ryker to the dance floor so they could show off their fiery salsa moves. Then Ryker danced with his mom, and Charlotte after that. A slow song came on for the fourth dance, and he found himself face to face with Wes again. Ryker couldn't help but laugh at the shocked expression on Wes's face.

"Where did you learn to dance like that?" Wes asked as they slowly came together. "What other secrets are you hiding?"

"It's not a secret. I never mentioned, you never asked, and we've never had the opportunity to go dancing," Ryker replied with a smirk. "My mom taught us. Dancing is a big part of Puerto Rican culture."

"Hmm, well, we definitely have to go out dancing from now on. Maybe you can teach me how to move like that," Wes said as he squeezed Ryker's hips.

"You've already got excellent rhythm, so no problem there," Ryker replied with a sultry stare.

"All of Me" began to play, and Wes and Ryker swayed together slowly among the other couples on the dance floor. Ryker remembered the song from the first night they spent together. He nuzzled his cheek against Wes's as their bodies moved in a sensuous tangle. Had it really been only a month since they'd met? It felt like their souls had known each other forever.

As the song neared its end, Wes stepped back and suddenly lowered himself to one knee.

Oh. My. God.

****

Wes

The plan had been to propose at the planetarium, but then it hit Wes as they were dancing. The song was right. The mood was right, and their family was there. This was the moment. So Wes went for it.

He bent down on one knee and took the ring box out of his pocket. His hands trembled as he looked up into those beautiful blue eyes that had claimed him from the very first glance.

"Ry, I know we've only been together a short time, but I am so in love with you, and I'm ready to start our life together. Right here. Right now. You knocked me on my ass the moment our eyes met, and I have yet to recover." He paused and licked his lips as the crowd *ooh-ed*, *ahh-ed*, and made the occasional whistle. "So here, in front of our family and friends, and surrounded by love, will you be my husband?" he asked, opening the box to show Ryker the two white gold bands he'd picked out.

There was silence in the room as Ryker stood there, tears slowly trickling down his stunning face as he mouthed, "Yes." Wes could barely hear it above the pounding of his own heart, but when the answer finally sank in, he rushed to his feet and bent Ryker back in a kiss so full of love and promise he never wanted it to end.

After a few minutes, Ryker pulled away. "Are you going to give me my ring?" he asked cheekily, and Wes rushed to place the gold band on his finger. Ryker took the other ring and slipped it onto Wes's left ring finger, then brought it to his mouth to place a kiss on it. "Love you," he murmured.

They were suddenly surrounded by their friends and family, Ryker's mom and sister both in tears. All of them offered hugs and excited congratulations.

"Fall wedding!" Luca yelled with both arms raised, and they all groaned.

"We just got engaged, man!" Wes protested as Ryker laughed.

As much as Wes enjoyed having their loved ones around, he wanted to be alone with Ryker. Now. Wes grabbed Ryker's hand and hauled him out into the hallway.

"Wes, where are we going? Oomph!"

Wes claimed Ryker's mouth in a kiss designed to drive him out of his mind. Their hot tongues dueled, and their bodies slid against each other as they moaned their enjoyment.

"I need you, right now," Wes whispered urgently against Ryker's swollen lips, pulling him into the bathroom and locking the door.

Fifteen minutes later, they emerged with their ties undone, their shirts half unbuttoned, their hair a mess, and their smiles so wide, it hurt. The jeers and whistles that greeted them when they reentered the ballroom caused Ryker to blush and Wes to bow. They quickly headed back to the dance floor to join their group.

"You know, we still have a book—well, several books—to finish. Are you sure you want to be stuck living *and* working with a grumpy, sarcastic writer who's set in his ways?" Ryker asked as he wrapped his arms around Wes's neck and swayed to the music.

Wes smiled as he rested their foreheads together, looking deep into Ryker's blue depths. "As long as you're okay sharing your life with a slightly egotistical, albeit super sexy, author who has bouts of writer's block," he replied, softly kissing Ryker's lips.

"No worries," Ryker whispered and kissed him back. "I have just the cure."

Epilogue

Luca

Five Months Later

The air was crisp today. Golden leaves swayed and fluttered in the breeze, a warm explosion of color against a cloudless blue sky. It was a perfect fall day for a wedding in Central Park.

Two men stood on the edge of Bow Bridge, the ornate iron railing providing a stunning architectural backdrop for their finest tuxedos. They were surrounded by a small group of family and friends, as well as three well-behaved dogs wearing matching bow ties.

The wedding was just as Luca had imagined it: simple and elegant, down to the very last detail. All the months of planning had been worth it.

Luca sighed as he watched his friend Wes marry the love of his life. Wes and Ryker had different personalities, but complemented each other in a way that Luca envied. With just a look or a quick touch, so much was said between the two men that anyone near them could see how much love and respect they had for one another. They'd only met six months ago, but it was love at first sight, and now they were married and starting a new life together in New York City. That was what Luca dreamed to have for himself one day.

He turned his attention from Wes to the red-haired man standing beside Ryker—tall and imposing in a trim navy-blue suit. Mac Duran. CEO. Socialite. Asshole. The sun lit up his fiery hair, making his piercing green eyes pop. Mac's square jaw was clenched, but he wore a small smile—the only sign of contentment on his sharp, angular face. Those eyes glanced in Luca's direction, and the intensity in them had Luca clenching his hands together. Then Mac's eyes narrowed, and Luca felt heat rise in his cheeks, despite the cool autumn weather. He would not back down and be the one to look away. He wasn't made like that. So he stood his ground until Mac finally relented and returned his attention to the couple saying their vows.

Luca took a deep breath and willed his body to relax. Mac's irritating effect on him was explosive, and he needed to get himself under control before he said something he'd regret. *Focus on the event at hand*, he reminded himself.

Once the ceremony was complete, everyone walked over to Uno, a nearby Italian eatery that was a favorite of the grooms. The private dining room provided a warm, intimate setting for their six-course menu of seafood, pasta, and a three-layer *dulce de leche* wedding cake that was covered in creamy white and navy-blue fondant and rust-colored roses. The effect was stunning, just like the duo of the day.

Ryker's mom, Tina, stood up after the first course and tapped a spoon against her glass. "Toast! Toast!"

Ryker and Wes got up to give their wedding speeches and thank-yous, and proceeded to make everyone jealous with their PDA.

Then it was the best man's turn. Mac got up and lifted his champagne flute.

"Congratulations to my best friend, Ryker, and his husband, Wes. When I suggested that Wes and Ryker collaborate on a book series, I envisioned a business relationship that would benefit both of them professionally." He paused and smiled. "But it turns out they got the better end of the deal when they fell in love with each other. Ryker, you are my oldest and dearest of friends, and I wish you and Wes a lifetime of love and happiness."

Luca was moved by Mac's heartfelt speech and, without thought, glanced up at him. When their eyes met, the usual spark of irritation intensified, and Luca felt his insides melt and his heart rate increase. He licked his lips involuntarily, and Mac's gaze roamed south.

Shit. Not good. You can't get hot for the Ice Man, he reminded himself.

When the speeches were over, Ryker pulled Luca aside.

"Thanks for staying in New York for the next couple of weeks to look after our fur babies."

"Of course. I have time to work on my event business, so it's a win-win."

"There is one other thing." Ryker hesitated. "Mac's assistant quit on him. Maybe you could help him out?"

"Stop right there. You know that Mac and I are like olive oil and ice water. Take a guess at who the ice water is." Luca paused. "Besides, there are HR agencies he can use. Come on, it's time for you to cut the cake." Ryker nodded and headed back to his husband.

Luca watched Wes and Ryker cut the wedding cake and playfully shove small pieces in each other's faces, laughing. Ryker's mother stood near Luca, watching and laughing along with them.

She nudged Luca's arm. "What a beautiful speech Mac gave, don't you agree?"

"It was. Who knew the Ice Man had a heart?" he murmured.

Tina's smile froze as she looked over Luca's shoulder. *Fuck.* He turned slowly to face the man himself.

"There's a lot you don't know," Mac snapped, then stalked off to the other side of the room.

So much for keeping his mouth shut.

The End

EVERNIGHT PUBLISHING ®

www.evernightpublishing.com